Gift from the

Storm

Rebekah A. Morris

Cover design by Perry Elisabeth Design
(perryelisabethdesign.blogspot.com)

Images ©Jorge Alonso and Daniel Korzeniewski | 123rf.com

ISBN: 1508768773
ISBN-13: 978-1508768777

Read Another Page Publishing

DEDICATION

My family who are always there for me when I write.
My mom, who reads my stories piecemeal and edits and
checks.
My sister, Sarah, who runs a continuous "sensibility check"
on all my stories as I write them.
My dad, who enjoys reading my books after they are
published.

CONTENTS

The fire crackled brightly in the fireplace of the Morgan cabin. Nestled in a hollow of the mountains where it was sheltered from many a fierce winter wind, the large, two-story house had stood for years. It wasn't really a cabin, but the Morgans loved to call it one since the outside was all logs. Inside was every modern convenience, including electricity. However, tonight only a few lamps burned in addition to the fire.

It was a pleasant group sitting about the rustic living room with its high vaulted ceiling and large picture windows. A walkway running from one side of the upstairs to the other looked down into the living room from either side of the large, stone chimney. Everywhere the house was dark save for the lamps and the fire in the living room where the family had gathered. Outside all was black, for the sun had long since set, and the air had an autumn chill to it. To those gathered about the cheerful blaze all was warm and peaceful, all thoughts of an earlier storm had vanished.

"Well, Justin, are you all settled in town?" Mr. Morgan, with his feet on a footstool, regarded his eldest son with a smile.

"I think so. Now that the water and electricity are hooked back up, the 'hospital' seems to be all set." Justin laughed as he said the word hospital.

"Hospital, yeah, right," eighteen-year-old Adam scoffed. "It was an old hotel and still looks like one. It even has the old name above the door."

"On the outside maybe," Justin countered good naturally, "but have you seen the inside?"

Adam shook his head.

"I haven't seen it either, Just." Sara settled herself more comfortably on the couch opposite her older brother. Her nut brown hair was loose about her shoulders and made her almost look her nineteen years. "But it will be nice to have one in town now, so we don't have to go all the way to Jackson."

"Since when have you ever been to a hospital?" Justin couldn't resist a little teasing.

Sara tossed her head. "Never. And I don't plan to go just because you are a doctor in this one."

"Oh, come on, Sis!" Justin pleaded. "Wouldn't you come visit me with a hot pie when I have been slaving away and am exhausted from all my multitude of patients?" He could be dramatic when he chose.

Pursing her lips, Sara pretended to give it some thought. "Maybe," she finally agreed, adding, "but I'd have to think about it first."

Justin threw a pillow at her which she promptly tossed back.

"But really, Son," Mrs. Morgan spoke softly when the pillows had ceased to fly, "I'm glad we now have a medical facility even if it does look like a hotel. As long as the personnel know what they are doing, that is what we need."

"Don't worry about that, Mother. There may not be

many of us, but I think we're ready. At least we'll do our best."

"That's all that needs done," Mr. Morgan agreed and then stared into the fire, and all fell silent.

The loud barking of their collie, Captain, broke the silence outside.

"What is he barking about?" Justin turned to try to look out the window behind him but could see nothing but the reflection of the fire and lamps.

"It's not his 'wild animal' bark nor is it his company coming bark—"

Adam stood up as Sara spoke and grabbed his shotgun from a rack nearby. "I'll go check."

"Be careful," Mrs. Morgan called.

In silence the rest of the family waited, listening to the barking which seemed to have a different tone to it than usual. Suddenly they were startled by Adam's cry, "Justin! Dad! Mother! Sara!"

The four sprang up and rushed for the door. There by the light of the front porch, which Mr. Morgan snapped on, they could see Adam supporting someone out in the yard. It was a young woman, and she was carrying something! In an instant the Morgan family were around them. The girl had two young children in her arms and was clearly exhausted.

"Here, Sara, take that one. Mother can you carry this one? Dad, steady her on this side. Get them inside while I grab my bag from the truck." Justin threw his orders rapidly and the next moment was sprinting the short distance to his pickup.

Moments later, he was back in the house. Flipping the lights on in the living room he found the girl sitting in a chair by the fire. Her eyes held a glazed look, while dark circles under them gave added proof that she hadn't slept for a while. She seemed on the verge of collapse.

"Just!"

Justin turned to find Sara holding a small child in her arms while tears trickled down her cheeks. She looked pleadingly at him. Motioning her to sit down, he jerked out his stethoscope. As he pulled back the tattered shirt the child was wrapped in, he noticed the bluish tint to its lips and the thin little arms. A quick check showed it was still alive.

Pulling a flannel throw off the back of a nearby rocking chair, he quickly wrapped it around the child. "Mother, I want some warm milk as quickly as possible."

With a nod Mrs. Morgan placed the other child in Adam's arms and hurried off.

This one, a child of about three years of age, began to cry, whether from cold, hunger or fright, no one knew.

"Danny," a dry hoarse voice called, "it's going to be okay."

The girl in the chair seemed to have been roused from her stupor by the crying and now held out her arms. "I'll take him."

"Let me keep him a little longer," Adam urged gently. "See, he has already quieted." It was true; as soon as he had heard his name, Danny had quit crying and now lay motionless in the strong arms that held him.

Quickly Justin examined him, and when the warm milk arrived, he gently forced some between the blue lips of the child in Sara's arms. Then turning to Danny, he offered him the cup. Eagerly the child drank it, holding it out for more when it was gone.

"You can have more later," Justin assured him.

"Mother, could you, Sara, and Adam give them baths and find clean clothes?"

Mrs. Morgan nodded.

"Then make sure they're wrapped up warmly and bring them back."

Again his mother nodded and said, "I'm sure some of the grandkids' clothes will fit. It's a good thing Heather keeps some extra things here. Come on Sara, Adam."

Before they could leave the room, however, the girl in the chair began looking frantically around, calling in hoarse tones, "Danny! Jenny! . . . Have to find them." Her restless hands tried to push off the blanket Mr. Morgan had tucked around her. "Jenny! Danny!" A violent fit of coughing put an end to her calls though she still struggled faintly to move from the chair.

"Easy there," Justin coaxed, taking one of her cold, shaking hands in his and noting her pulse. "Everything is going to be all right. Just relax." Gently he kept her from getting up, talking soothingly all the while. "Danny and Jenny are going to be all right. They are being taken care of, don't worry about them."

Mr. Morgan handed Justin a glass of warm milk. Adding a few drops from a bottle he pulled from his medical bag, Justin dropped down in front of the chair. "Here," he said, holding it to the girl's lips, "drink this."

For a moment she sat limp and made no move to do as she was told. Her eyelids drooped.

"Come on," Justin ordered softly, "drink it."

Obediently her mouth opened and she took a swallow.

"What is your name?"

The words or the tone seemed to penetrate the fog

that surrounded her mind for she sighed and straightened. "Who are you?" she asked in a bewildered way.

Justin had shifted to one knee before her where he could watch every expression of her face with his keen eyes. "I'm Doctor Justin Morgan. What is your name?"

"Amy." The name was murmured, and she shivered, moaning as she did so while an expression of pain flitted over her pale face.

"Amy, can you tell me what hurts?"

No answer came.

A few more swallows from the cup revived her enough to mumble, "My leg," before relapsing into the stupor from which it was so hard to pull her.

After handing Mr. Morgan the cup, Justin pulled back the blanket. A quick examination brought a frown to Justin's face and he looked up at his dad. "I don't like this," he admitted frankly. "If it weren't so dark and cold, I'd take all three down to the hospital at once. As it is,—" Breaking off abruptly, he again felt the girl's pulse and laid his hand against her hot face. "I don't want them exposed to any more of that cold air now."

Mr. Morgan nodded. "Do you want her in the upstairs or downstairs bedroom?"

"Down."

"Then I'll go open the door and the vent so it will warm up."

"Justin," Sara spoke softly as she entered the living room a little while later.

Rising from the floor, Justin turned. "Hmm, what we need is a baby bottle. I don't think that little one is going to drink much if we try a cup or spoon." He was looking down into the small, pinched face of the tiny girl in his sister's arms.

"I have a bottle somewhere. Do you want it?"

"You have one? Where?"

"In my room."

"Get it," Justin ordered, taking the child himself. "It will have to be sterilized."

Sara nodded and disappeared.

Before she returned, Mrs. Morgan and Adam, with a sleepy, little Danny, came back. Danny, after Justin gave him a quick examination, was made happy by another cup of milk and then carried off to bed. Several minutes later, Sara carried Jenny and the bottle of milk up to her room, Justin promising to come up later.

Mrs. Morgan now laid a hand on her son's arm. "What about her?" She nodded towards the chair near the fireplace.

Justin sighed. "I want to take her to the hospital, but not tonight in this weather. Dad is warming up a guest room down the hall."

"Do you know her name?"

"Amy."

"That's it?"

"That's it. Frankly, Mother, all I know is her first name, that she has a badly injured and infected leg and a terrible cough, and is on the brink of total collapse. I'm guessing she's about eighteen, but that's just a guess."

"The poor girl!" Together the two of them stood looking down on the white, pain-filled face of the stranger before them. The light of the flames danced across the thin hand and arm which hung limp and still over the arm of the chair.

"The room is ready." The softly spoken words

brought Justin into action. Together with his father, they lifted and carried the girl in and laid her on the bed. Once there, Justin made a more careful examination of her leg, forced a spoonful of medicine between her unwilling lips and, tucking a hot water bottle in beside her, drew the covers up. Leaving only a small lamp on, he slipped out into the hall.

It was a long night for the young doctor so recently out of medical school who, with keeping an eye on the two little ones upstairs and Amy downstairs, got very little sleep. Yet, the early light of the new dawn filtering in through the office windows found him on the phone with the newly formed hospital in town.

"Yes, . . . I want immediate x-rays of the leg . . . Dr. Stern should be alerted for consultation later . . . No—complete check on both little ones . . . Have no idea at present . . . Sounds good. Thanks."

~2~

"Dr. Morgan, the x-rays are ready whenever you want them."

Justin glanced up from a chart. "Thanks, Stacy. I'll be right there."

For a moment, Dr. Justin Morgan continued to study the chart in his hand, then, with a slight frown, he set it back down, glanced at his watch and left the office. Striding down the narrow hallway he soon reached another room where a young intern was adjusting an x-ray on a screen.

"Well, Philips, what does it look like?"

The young man turned. "Not bad, Dr. Morgan," he replied. "A slight fracture right here." He pointed to the screen before him.

For some time only the low murmur of their voices could be heard as together the young intern and the nearly as young doctor studied the pictures. At last, Justin turned away remarking, "I'll be back later when Dr. Stern comes. I think you're right about the bone having only a slight break, but I don't like the look of the leg."

Dr. Morgan started back down the hall stifling a yawn. He would go check on the babies and Amy and then perhaps he could catch a few winks of sleep. Dr. Stern would get here when he could, but it was a good two or three hour drive from Jackson to this small mountain town.

Justin took the stairs two at a time from the old hotel lobby to the second floor. Though the hotel had been changed into a hospital, the former lobby with all its gilt and trim had been kept much the same. It had always been a dream of Justin Morgan to start a hospital in his home town, and for this he had worked hard, gathering to his side as staff and hospital personnel, other doctors, interns and nurses. When no property could be had cheap enough to build a hospital, Mr. Morgan had suggested to his son the renovation of the old hotel which had been vacated only a few years before for a newer one closer to the highway. This had met with approval and the work had begun. When Dr. Stern, a successful doctor in the prime of life, heard of this new venture, he volunteered his services as consulting physician for anything Dr. Morgan and his staff couldn't handle. This offer greatly boosted Justin's idea from dream into reality.

Now, nearly six months from the start of the project, the hospital was complete and even had its first three patients.

As Dr. Morgan approached Room 207, he could hear laughing. Wondering, he opened the door to find little Danny flirting with two nurses.

"What is going on here?"

The nurses turned. "He won't sleep, Doctor," one of them offered.

"After a good nap earlier and a good meal, he seems ready to go," the second nurse put in. "Neither of us can get the little tyke to stop playing."

Dr. Morgan couldn't help a slight smile at the little

fellow who gazed up at him out of large blue eyes and then gave a crooked grin. "How old are you, Danny?" he asked, glancing at the chart by his bed.

With another impish grin at the two nurses, little Danny held up three fingers.

"Why, Dr. Morgan," Nurse Franklin exclaimed, "how did you get him to tell? We've tried several times, and he never would tell us how old he is."

"The child recognizes an authority figure when he sees one," was the reply in pretended haughty tones, but with a pleased look at Danny.

Danny giggled as his temperature was taken and then snuggled down with a sleepy look. Dr. Morgan regarded him in silence until the blue eyes closed and he fell asleep. Then, turning to the nurses, he spoke softly.

"He still has a bit of a fever. One of you keep an eye on him and let me know when he wakes up."

With that he left the room.

Across the hall, he entered a second room. There he found Jenny sleeping under the careful eye of Nurse Allen.

At his questioning she said, "Her fever is still high, but she seems to have perked up more after the last feeding."

"Good. I wonder how old she is?" This last was almost to himself.

"I can't say for sure, Doctor, but I'd guess she's about ten months."

With a nod and a promise to return later, he continued his rounds.

It was in Room 212 that he stopped next. The shades were drawn so as to let in only a little light which fell upon the still figure in the white bed.

"Any change?" this was asked of the older nurse sitting by the bed.

She shook her head. "None, sir. She just lies here without moving except for moaning and tossing her head."

"Can you get any liquid down her?"

Again Nurse Jones shook her head. "Not much. Only a swallow now and then."

"Well, keep trying. I think we'll have to start an IV just to get liquid in her, if she doesn't respond soon." As he spoke, Dr. Morgan glanced at the bandage on her leg. He was trying to decide if he should look at it now or wait, when a soft knock was heard on the door.

Stepping across the room, Justin opened it.

"Dr. Stern just arrived, sir," Intern Philips whispered.

"Thanks. I'll be right down." A few quiet instructions to the nurse and then Justin hurried down to the lobby.

"Dr. Stern, I'm glad you're here. You certainly made good time." The young doctor greeted the veteran with a hearty handshake. "I hope this call didn't interrupt anything too important."

With a smile Dr. Stern replied, "Only my morning nap." Then looking keenly at Dr. Morgan, he added, "You look as though you missed yours."

"Don't remind me," Justin begged. "But come," he added, suddenly businesslike, "and I'll fill you in."

Leading the way to his own office, the two doctors remained closeted there for nearly half an hour.

"This is the X-ray of her leg. As you can see here," and Dr. Morgan pointed, "there seems to be a slight fracture of the bone."

Dr. Stern nodded. "Yes, I can see that, though it

doesn't look serious."

"I agree," Justin sighed. "But I'm quite concerned about the infection in her leg."

"Suppose I take a look now."

Soon the two doctors were walking along the hall. "This is quite a set-up you have here," Dr. Stern remarked, admiring the gilt and trim in the lobby.

Justin gave a chuckle. "No one would guess this was a hospital from the outside or the lobby."

"It's not the looks that matter, it's the work done inside that counts."

"That's what my mother says," agreed Justin. "Here we are." His voice hushed as he opened the door to the room where Amy lay.

Nurse Jones looked up. "No change," she said softly.

Dr. Morgan nodded. Swiftly removing the bandage on the injured leg, he stepped back so that Dr. Stern might take a look.

"The other thing I'm concerned about, sir," Justin continued, after the leg had been examined and suggestions offered by Dr. Stern, "is her condition otherwise."

It was afternoon by the time Dr. Stern left the hotel turned hospital. Dr. Morgan followed him out to his car. "I think you're on the right track with the girl's treatment," Dr. Stern remarked, opening his car door. "There's not much a person can do except wait for them to wake up."

"Thank you, sir, for coming out." Dr. Justin held out his hand. "I feel more confident having talked things over with you."

With a smile, Dr. Stern shook the offered hand. "Glad

I could help out. And Justin," he added, using for the first time the young doctor's first name, "please don't hesitate to call me any time day or night. Even if you just want a second opinion about something, give me a ring."

"I will, sir. Thanks again."

Dr. Stern gave a wave, backed out onto the road and headed out of town.

Turning back to the hospital, Justin suddenly felt exhausted. He had been up since six o'clock yesterday morning and it was now nearly two the following afternoon. "I'll grab a bite to eat and then, . . . no." He shook his head. "Philips," he called to the young intern coming down the hall.

"Yes, sir?"

"I'm going to go take a nap in my office. Wake me up if there is any change in any of the patients or if I'm needed for anything."

The intern nodded, and Justin turned to his office. There he had fixed a cot for just such a time, though he had wondered if he would ever need it. Now he was thankful it was there. Stumbling over to it, he sank down and was asleep before his head touched the pillow.

"Dr. Morgan!"

Justin heard his name called and felt someone shaking his shoulder. For a moment he couldn't remember where he was.

"Dr. Morgan," the voice persisted.

Suddenly it all came back to him. His eyes flew open and he sat up quickly. "I'm awake Philips. What is it?"

Andrew Philips stepped back from the cot now that Justin was awake. "It's the girl in 212, sir. She's delirious, and Nurse Jones sent me for you."

"Thanks." That was all Justin said, but as he sprang up, grabbed his jacket and headed for the door, he gave his young intern a quick hand clasp before rushing for the stairs.

Up in Room 212, Dr. Morgan discovered his patient muttering and talking, trying to feebly push back the covers, turning her head restlessly while the nurse stood beside the bed trying to soothe and calm her.

"There, there, Child," Nurse Jones took one of the thin hands in her own. "Everything will be all right. Just go to sleep now."

"No!" Amy exclaimed, her eyes bright with fever and her lips parched. "I can't let them go! No, they are mine! Why are you here?" She demanded of Dr. Morgan when she caught sight of him. "You're dead. No one lived. You're an impostor!"

The doctor and nurse exchanged glances. What was she talking about? Would her wild talk tell them anything about who she was or who the children were? Was she their mother? She looked too young for that, yet . . .

"Amy," Dr. Morgan spoke quietly, placing a hand on her burning face and then laying steady fingers on her wrist. "I'm Dr. Morgan. Everything is going to be all right now."

For a moment the girl stared at him, then in pitiful, pleading tones she begged as she clutched his hand, "Oh, please, don't let anyone take them from me. She was . . . the sister I never had," and her lips trembled though her eyes remained dry.

"No one is going to take anything from you," Justin assured, nodding to the nurse. "Now drink this for me, won't you?" he coaxed, raising her head and holding a glass to her lips.

After a swallow or two, Amy turned her head away, saying in a complete change of tone, "Of course they're only paper dolls. It doesn't matter. Nothing matters—any more." Her eyes closed and she lay still. Her watchers scarcely dared to breathe, hoping she had fallen asleep. That hope was a vain one, for half a minute later a cough shook the thin form and the large, dark, fever filled eyes opened. "Matt," she whispered between coughs, "don't forget . . . the others." She clutched Dr. Morgan's hand, breathing rapidly. "You won't . . . forget?"

"I won't. Now go to sleep," Justin replied quietly, remaining where he was while his keen eyes watched his patient.

This time the eyes did close in sleep. Not a refreshing, strength renewing sleep, only a sleep of exhaustion.

And thus began the long, tedious hours. Hours which turned into days and nights all running together. There were days when no one could calm the girl who had appeared so suddenly from the mountains, days when she clung to Dr. Morgan, calling him Matt and crying for Kathleen, days when the fever filled eyes swam with tears and she kept sobbing over and over, "No, no, no!"

Dr. Morgan fought the fever with all the knowledge and skill he possessed, seeking advice from Dr. Stern who came out every other day, and praying constantly. Never had he been faced with a situation quite like this before. He scarcely slept, except in snatches here and there. His eating was as irregular as his sleeping. How it would all end, he didn't know.

~ *3* ~

The two little ones who had arrived with the exhausted Amy had both been released from the hospital and were staying with the Morgans. All had been hoping that Danny would be able to tell them a few things, but aside from asking for "Maimie" for the first few days, he seemed to accept his new life without a thought as to what it had been before.

One day when Heather, the oldest child in the Morgan family, was visiting her parents with her three small children, she remarked to Sara, "Danny and Jenny are so cute, I wonder what their story is."

"You and all the rest of us," Sara sighed, looking down at the blanket on the floor where Jenny was trying to decide if she would go to sleep.

"How's Justin doing?" Heather asked next.

Sara shrugged. "I haven't seen him since they came."

Heather looked surprised. "Haven't you been down to the hospital?"

"No, Mother has gone but I've stayed with the little ones."

For several minutes Heather was silent. Then she

stood up. "Let's both go down."

"And leave the babies?"

"My Lucas is sleeping and Jenny is almost asleep. I'm sure Mother and Adam won't mind keeping an eye on the others. Come on," she coaxed. "We'll take Justin some of the pie you just made."

At that Sara laughed. "Okay, if Mother agrees to watch the others.

Mrs. Morgan readily agreed and the sisters departed with more than a piece of pie for their brother.

Arriving at the hospital, Heather looked up at the name carved into the stone above the door. "I haven't been in this place since it was a hotel."

"Me either." Sara said, then amending her statement added, "I mean I haven't been here since the renovations have been finished."

In the lobby they met Justin coming down the stairs. His shoulders sagged and he looked worn out, but his face brightened when he saw his sisters. "Hi," he greeted them.

"You look almost ready to drop," Heather told him after a hug.

Giving a tired smile, he sighed.

"How is she?" Sara asked, rightly reading more than tiredness in his face.

"Amy? I left her sleeping with Nurse Franklin on watch since I had to send Mrs. Jones home to rest. She was more worn out than I am. I just came down to grab a bite of something."

"Well, we got here at just the right time then," Heather smiled, taking the basket from her younger sister. "Care for a piece of fresh apple pie?"

For answer Justin sat down on the lowest step and reached for the basket. His sisters watched him eat

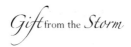

hungrily while they told him about the children. At last he stood up. "Thanks. That will keep me going for a while."

"Justin," Sara asked hesitatingly, "Can we . . . I mean would we be allowed to . . ."

Understanding her unfinished questions, he nodded. "If you want to see her, come on up. Her fever isn't contagious."

Silently Sara and Heather followed their brother up the steps and down the quiet hall. Pausing at the door, they waited while Justin told them softly, "If Amy is awake, don't be surprised if she tells you to go away. One minute she hates me and the next tells me I'm the only one who loves her." He made a slight face.

With the opening of the door, he instantly became Dr. Morgan again, not just Justin. His sisters noticed the change and felt a new respect for him. Never had they seen him in his role as a physician in a hospital and both halted instinctively just inside the door.

"Matt!" the voice, pleading and weak, came from the bed as Dr. Justin approached. "Where's Kathleen? Where is she?" There was a frantic, hysterical tone in the voice and Amy clutched his arm like a drowning person clutches a life preserver.

"Shh," Dr. Morgan soothed, "Kathleen's all right—"

He got no farther for, as he moved closer to the bed, the feverish eyes of the girl rested on the two in the doorway. With a glad cry, Amy held out shaking arms. "Kathleen!"

After a quick glance at Heather, Sara took a step towards the bed. Was she calling her?

But Amy's arms fell down and she whimpered, "I want Kathleen."

19

"Heather," Dr. Morgan spoke low. He nodded towards the bed and swiftly Heather came over.

"I'm right here, Dear," she comforted, brushing back the girl's light hair from her hot face. "There's no need to fret, just relax and go to sleep now."

"Everything's all right?"

"Perfectly all right. Now I want you to drink this for me." Gently lifting Amy's head, Heather held the glass Justin had pushed into her hand, to the girl's lips. "That's right. There now, just close your eyes and get some sleep."

"You won't leave me, will you?" Amy murmured.

"No, Dear, I can stay for a while." And, after glancing swiftly at her brother and seeing the chair he had quietly placed beside the bed, Heather sat down.

"Sing," begged the weary voice from the bed.

Knowing she wasn't a very good singer, Heather hesitated a moment. Sara and Justin were the singers of the family, they should sing. Besides, what does one sing to someone so ill? How could she sing before these others? These thoughts flashed through her mind as well as a quick prayer for help. Focusing all her attention on the girl in the bed, Heather smiled. "I'll sing if you will close your eyes and try to sleep."

Obediently Amy closed her eyes although she kept a tight grip on Heather's hand.

"God, that madest earth and heaven,
Darkness and light;
Who the day for toil hast given,
For rest the night;"

The restless fingering of the bed clothes by Amy's free hand ceased as the haunting melody reached her ears and penetrated to her brain.

"May Thy angel guards defend us,
Slumber sweet Thy mercy send us;
Holy dreams and hopes attend us
This live-long night."

Softly the song slipped into the quiet room, filling it with a stillness, a peace and a calm, that seemed to hush even the troubled thoughts of Dr. Morgan, for as he watched his patient's breathing grow steady, saw her rigid form grow limp under the blanket, his face, which had been so tense, relaxed and he leaned against the wall; his shoulders dropped, letting the simple, well known song speak peace and calm to every fiber of his being.

"And when morn again shall call us
To run life's way,
May we still whatever befall us,
Thy will obey."

Heather sang all the verses before she stopped, and, when Amy didn't move, she looked up at her brother.

"Can you stay here?" he whispered, bending down so that his lips were close to her ear.

Raising her eyebrows in surprise, she shrugged. "I suppose so," she replied softly. "But, what about the children, Timothy . . ."

"I'll take care of that if you'll only stay!"

Seeing the look of pleading on his tired face, Heather could only nod.

Motioning the nurse, Dr. Morgan moved on cat's feet

to the door where Sara still stood watching.

Out in the hall, he spoke in a low voice to Nurse Franklin for a minute before starting towards the lobby with his sister; their footsteps sounded strangely loud after the stillness of the sick room.

Turning to her as they stepped down the last step, he yawned. "Sara," he began, "I need your help."

"It looks like you need Heather's help, not mine," Sara replied, not feeling the least bit of jealousy, for nursing was not in her line.

"I need both," he clarified. "She has been the only one who has been able to quiet her so quickly. Of course I don't know if she'll be able to do it again, but I don't dare risk her not being here when she wakes up."

Nodding her head, Sara gave a snort. "You really should go to bed, Just. Your pronouns are as clear as mud."

"I know. Then you'll help me?"

"I'll watch the children, if that is what you want. Should I call Timothy, too, and let him know he can't have his wife back for a while?"

Justin looked relieved. "Would you, Sara? I have to get some sleep while she's sleeping. I can hardly function right now."

With a grin, Sara gave her brother a push towards his office and ordered, "Go on and get to bed. I'll make the call for you."

Everything was dark when Justin awoke, dark and quiet. Feeling much refreshed by his nap, he turned a lamp on and glanced at his watch. It was nearly midnight! Surely Amy hadn't been asleep this whole time. Was Heather still here? Why hadn't anyone wakened him? Quickly he slipped out into the hall and up the stairs.

The room was dim and hushed. Heather still sat beside the bed one hand clasped in Amy's. Silently Justin slipped over and laid quiet fingers on his patient's wrist. The pulse was faint but steady. A soft sigh escaped him as he felt the girl's forehead and discovered it was cool and damp.

"Thank God!" he breathed, feeling hope for the stranger's life for the first time in days. "The fever has broken."

"Just." The voice was a soft whisper and Dr. Morgan looked across the bed to find his sister watching him. He returned her anxious look with a smile and watched the tense line of her shoulders loosen.

Slipping as silently out of the room as he had slipped into it, Dr. Morgan hurried to find Nurse Allen and soon the two of them returned. The nurse took up her post beside the bed while Heather, gently sliding her hand from the now relaxed hold which had held it so fast, moved to the door.

Not a word was spoken as she followed her brother out of the room and down to the lobby where he pulled up two chairs and, sinking into one, asked, "What happened?"

Heather shrugged. "Not much. She woke up a few times, tightened her hold on my hand and asked me to sing again. I didn't notice any change until you came in. She's going to be all right?"

Giving a deep sigh, he nodded. "It looks like it. Maybe we'll be able to find out who she is when she wakes up again. Thank God you were here!"

The two tired workers exchanged smiles. "What should I do now?" Heather wondered. "I can sit with her the rest of the night if you want. As long as Timothy knows where I am." She added the last more as a question, than a statement.

"He should. Sara said she'd call him. I don't know if you should sit with her. It wouldn't hurt, but are you sure you're up to it?" Dr. Morgan yawned.

"I'm more up for it than you seem to be." Heather laid her hand on her brother's arm. "Just tell me what I should do, and then you can go get some more sleep."

It was mid-morning when Amy opened her eyes and looked about her. Where in the world was she? What had happened and why did she feel so tired? Someone turned and a hand was placed on her wrist, but no one said a word. Moving her eyes slowly about, she discovered two other persons in the room as well. One was dressed in white while the other was wearing browns. Bewildered, she looked back at the face above her and asked weakly, "Who are you?"

Dr. Morgan, his keen eyes taking in every look, every movement of his patient, replied quietly, "I'm Dr. Justin Morgan. What is your name?"

"Amy," came the slow reply while the girl's eyes drifted to the half closed blinds at the window.

Quietly watching and waiting, Dr. Morgan soon realized the girl was still too weak and tired to be able to think much. Except for her eyes taking in the room with its silent occupants, she didn't move, not even her head. "Amy," the name was soft. "Swallow this for me, please."

Slowly the large, dark eyes focused themselves on Dr. Morgan's face and then moved to the spoon he was holding, but she made no movement. It seemed too much of an effort to even open her mouth. The four words she had spoken had taken all of her strength. Lying there limp, only her eyes moved, and it was an effort to keep them open.

Justin gently raised her head and held the spoon to her lips. "Come on," he coaxed. "That's right," as the lips parted almost of themselves and the liquid slipped in. "Now swallow it, Amy."

With great effort the eyes moved to the face above her and met Dr. Morgan's blue ones.

"Swallow," his voice was quiet but compelling and as though just comprehending what he said, she obeyed. Then her eyes closed as her head was laid back on the snow white pillow, and she slept.

Rebekah A. Morris

~ 4 ~

All that day and the next Amy was listless, asked no more questions and only ate or drank when told to. She slept a great deal; real sleep this time, restful, strength renewing sleep. Dr. Morgan didn't push her to talk, he knew that would come later as her strength returned.

Finally, on the third day after the fever left, Amy was watching the door when Dr. Morgan entered her room. Her expression was half frightened and half bewildered. No one else was there.

"What is it, Amy?" Dr. Morgan asked quietly.

"Did I—" she hesitated. "I mean when someone found me were there two . . ." her lip quivered and her eyes pleaded for help.

"There were two little ones, and they are just fine."

Sighing as though a load had been rolled from her shoulders, Amy turned her eyes to the window. "I knew I had them with me, but I don't remember being found or what happened to them." Turning back she asked, "Where are they?"

Justin smiled, "Don't worry about them, they are safe and well. My parents and brother and sister are taking care of them." Justin sat down beside the bed, wondering if now would be a good time to find out more of who his patient was. He didn't have to ask, for Amy, assured that the two children were safe, had to talk.

"How did I get here? The last thing I remember was seeing a light and hoping I could get the children down to it."

"You did make it. It was to my family's house and our dog found you."

"We had been so long in the mountains. I know I got the children out of something and started walking, but I don't know what it was." Her face was puzzled. "I keep trying to remember, and I can't." She had begun twisting the top of the sheet between her fingers.

"Don't try," Dr. Morgan advised. "It will probably all come back to you before long, but don't try to hurry it."

There were a few minutes of quiet. Amy lay staring at the wall and Dr. Morgan watched her. At last he spoke. His voice was quiet and calm.

"Amy, are you the children's mother?"

Turning startled eyes to the doctor's face, she gasped, "Oh, no! I'm not their mother!"

"There's no need to get excited, Amy," Justin assured her. "When you came you only told us your first names, so we have wondered."

"I'm Amy Jones and they are . . . they . . . I don't know!" Her voice rose, her hands twisted the sheet again. "Doctor, I don't know who they are!"

"Shh," Dr. Morgan soothed, chiding himself for getting her excited. "You are tired. It is hard to remember things when one is tired. Now no more talking," he said as Amy's lips parted. "I want you to drink this and then go to sleep. You have talked quite enough for now."

Amy slowly settled back after swallowing the drink

she had been given. "Doctor—"

"Hush, I want you to rest now." Dr. Morgan closed the window shades, leaving the room dim.

But Amy had to know one thing. "Just their names, please!" she pleaded.

"Danny and Jenny. Now no more talking." He moved to the door but paused with it half open to watch the girl in the bed a moment.

"Poor girl," he sighed to himself. "I wonder how long it will be before she remembers. She had to get the children out of 'something'. I wonder what. A cabin? A car? Why did they have to get out?" Shaking his head, he made his way down to his office still pondering what she had said.

"Amy Jones. That's all I've got, Dad." There was a pause and Justin leaned his head on his hand. "How are you supposed to find the right Amy Jones? . . . No idea . . . Nope. She doesn't remember what she had to get the children out of but it was in the mountains . . . Yeah, that's what I was wondering . . . Several days at least, I'm guessing. I doubt if she'd even know, if she could remember." There was another pause. Longer this time. "Yep, I will . . . Thanks Dad. Bye."

For several minutes, Justin sat at his desk, leaning his head on his hand, lost in thought. Heaving a deep sigh, he stretched and then relaxed against the back of the chair, glancing at the open door to see intern Philips leaning against the door frame watching him. He grinned.

"Am I wanted for anything, Philips?"

Philips shook his head. "No, sir. Why don't you get out of the hospital for a few days? We haven't had many patients, and Amy is on the mend."

"No, I can't leave now, thanks though." Justin shook his head. "I'm all right. I should get more sleep now."

Philips, seeing that Dr. Morgan was determined to remain, could only nod and walk away.

For several minutes Justin busied himself with his paperwork and, when a knock sounded, he lifted his head and glanced towards the open door. "Wright, come on in. Have a seat," he invited cordially as the hospital surgeon, and his good friend, paused in the doorway.

"Do you have a few minutes?" he asked.

"Sure. Paperwork can wait," and Dr. Morgan pushed the papers to one side.

Instead of sitting, Dr. Wright leaned down to cross his arms on the back of the chair before the desk. Eyeing his colleague for a moment before he spoke, the surgeon frowned thoughtfully. "Morgan," he began quickly. "You need a break. You should get out of this hospital and do something relaxing for a change."

Justin laughed. "That's what Philips was just saying. I'm all right. I'll take a break later."

Dr. Wright straightened and gripped the chair back. "Look," he said, "ever since that girl arrived you've worked day and night, catching sleep and food here and there, hit and miss. You need a break, even if only for a few hours. No," he put up his hand as Justin was about to speak. "Let me finish. We've all talked about it and there is no reason why you can't get away for a few hours. Philips is quite capable of filling in for you until your return, and Hollend, Douglas and I can handle the few people who might come in. I'm serious, Morgan; you need to get out. Go up to your family's and have supper, spend the evening, the night if you will. Then come back refreshed."

Dr. Morgan sat in silence for some time after Dr.

Wright finished. His brows furled in thought while he fiddled with a pen. "I really—"

"Should go," a new voice finished his sentence and Dr. Douglas entered the room followed by Dr. Hollend.

Surveying his three fellow physicians, Dr. Morgan chuckled. "You sure know how to get the job done, don't you? What would you do if I still said no?"

Dr. Hollend crossed his arms with a smile. "Well, we've talked about handcuffs and delivering you to your father with instructions to keep you for twenty-four hours."

At that Justin laughed. "You win. I'll leave as soon as I finish this last paper."

"How soon will that be?"

"Ten or fifteen minutes at most, I'd guess."

"We'll hold you to it," Dr. Wright slapped the desk. "So get busy."

Breathing deeply of the brisk mountain air, Justin shut the door of his truck and stood for a minute just gazing about him at the bare trees, the tawny grass, the rocky cliffs, an eagle soaring overhead in the pale blue sky; all so peaceful, so quiet, so calming. Slowly he strolled to the front door. He hadn't realized how much he needed to get away until now. It was good to be out of the four walls of that hospital.

Justin found Adam and Sara in the living room playing with Danny and Jenny.

"Hi." Sara looked up to greet him.

"Hi," Justin smiled at his brother who was attempting to sit up while Danny sat on his stomach. "New way to exercise, Adam?" he chuckled.

"Yeah," Adam grunted falling back to the floor.

"How's Amy?" Sara questioned.

"She was sleeping when I left. I already told Dad all that she told me."

Sara nodded. "And he told us. Didn't know if there was anything new."

Justin shook his head as his mother entered the room.

"I see they really did kick you out," she remarked as he kissed her. "When Alex Wright called this morning saying you were going to have supper with us, I wasn't sure I believed him."

"But she cooked enough for you anyway," Sara put in.

Justin sat down, remarking, "I don't know if I'll be able to get up again." The couch was soft and comfortable and, kicking off his shoes just as he used to do, he stretched out with a sigh. "Let me know when supper's ready if I fall asleep."

"Don't you dare go to sleep now, Justin Morgan," Sara ordered. "You can sleep in your own bed tonight, but we haven't seen you for a long time. What if we want to talk?" She threw the pillow she had been leaning on at her brother and he turned on his side and tucked it under his head.

"Talk away. I'm not asleep yet."

Mrs. Morgan had returned to the kitchen and the three young people fell to talking. Soon Mr. Morgan returned home and Danny ran to meet him, letting Adam move from the floor to a chair.

"Welcome home, Justin," Mr. Morgan greeted his son. "You are staying the night, aren't you?"

"Thanks, Dad. I wasn't planning on it—"

"Well, plan on it then," his father interrupted bluntly. "I just talked with Dr. Douglas. He said they'd call you if you were needed before nine tomorrow morning."

Justin sat up. "Nine o'clock?" His face was filled with disbelief. "I was planning on returning by nine tonight!"

Before anything else could be said on the subject, supper was announced.

Rebekah A. Morris

~5~

The hot, home-cooked meal was a delight to Justin who hadn't left the hospital long enough to eat anything except what was brought to him, and that was usually cold or at least cool by the time he got around to eating it. The talk around the supper table, kept up by Sara and Adam, was about the two temporary additions to the family, or of Heather, Timothy and their children. All mention of the hospital with its unknown patient was ignored, as was the subject of Justin's return. It wasn't until the meal was over and dishes were washed, when all the members of the family were relaxing around the fireplace, that the subject was brought up.

Justin began it. "Dad, I don't know if I should stay the night." He wore an anxious expression.

"I think you should," replied his father quietly from where he sat with Danny looking at a book on his lap.

And Mrs. Morgan added, "It is only for a few hours, Son. You yourself said that Amy was doing better. You also said the staff at the hospital was qualified. Don't you think they can function without you?"

"When you put it that way, Mother, if I insisted on returning I'd sound like a . . . a . . . ." he fumbled for the right word.

"A politician," Sara finished for him.

Blinking in surprise, Justin glanced over at his brother. Did Adam know where she got that comparison?

Sara saw the looks exchanged and added, as she removed a piece of paper from Jenny's mouth, "Don't most politicians think that they know everything and act like nothing can get done without them?"

Her brothers broke into a laugh at that and even her parents chuckled. She certainly knew how to put things. When Justin could talk again, he assured her that now there was no way he was going back to the hospital before nine o'clock the next morning unless, he added, they called him.

"Good," Sara said, and stood up. "Won't you play with me now?"

With a yawn, Justin slowly arose from the couch. "If I can keep my eyes open enough to see the notes, I will."

Together they settled themselves, as they used to do, on the bench before the baby grand piano. After a quick scale or two, Justin declared he was ready and a lively waltz filled the room. Song followed song for some time; some lively and gay, some militant and grand, and some sweet and soothing. At last they stopped with a grand flourish.

"Would one of you play while we all sing the evening hymns?" Mrs. Morgan asked into the hush which followed the final march.

Sara slid off the bench quickly, saying quietly, "You play, Just."

Justin had no need of sheet music, for he had played those hymns so often in the years gone by that they were a part of him. Striking a few chords while the family gathered about, he then let his rich tenor lead them all in song while his fingers roved about the ivory keys drawing forth the sweet tunes.,

"Day is dying in the west;
Heaven is touching earth with rest:
Wait and worship while the night
Sets her evening lamps alight
Through all the sky."

One hymn followed another with scarcely a pause between, for all knew them and they were always sung in the same order.

"Abide with me: fast falls the even-tide;
The darkness deepens; Lord, with me abide:
When other helpers fail, and comforts flee,
Help of the helpless, O abide with me!"

Then the closing verse of the final hymn rang forth.

"Be near to bless me when I wake,
Ere thru the world my way I take;
Abide with me till in Thy love
I lose myself in heav'n above."

The hush which followed was broken by Mr. Morgan. "Let's have our evening prayer before certain some ones head to bed."

Justin, feeling more tired than he thought he should be, soon followed Danny and Jenny to bed and, before the clock struck nine, was so sound asleep that the noise Adam made coming to bed didn't disturb his dreams.

The air was chilly and clouds hung closely about the mountain tops. All around seemed hushed and shrouded in a damp, misty cloak which muted every sound. Pulling his coat tighter about himself, Justin drew in a lung full of the fresh, invigorating morning air. He felt rested, refreshed, ready for another day; the night away from the hospital had done him more good than he had thought possible. Now he was eager to get back.

As he climbed into his truck and started the engine, his thoughts were on his patient. How had Amy slept? Had she been able to remember any more? Who was she anyway?

Carefully driving down the rather steep mountain road, Justin forced his attention to his driving for, with the low clouds, seeing was difficult at any distance.

"You look like a new man, Morgan," Dr. Wright greeted Dr. Morgan with a hearty handshake. "Looks like my prescription worked."

Dr. Morgan smiled. "It sure did. I hadn't realized I was so worn out. How are things?"

"Slow. Haven't had a single new patient since you left."

"And Amy?"

Dr. Wright nodded towards the stairway where Philips was descending. "Ask him."

To his inquiry, intern Philips said that he had left Amy sleeping. She had slept most of the time since he had been gone. Yes, she had eaten a little; not much, but there was some improvement. No, she really hadn't said much at all.

"And how are Danny and Jenny doing, sir?" Philips wondered when he had finished his report on Amy.

"They both appear to be doing just fine. They are both filling out and my sister says Jenny is starting to crawl. I don't think we'll have to worry about them. But I'd feel better if I knew who they were."

* * *

"Dr. Morgan, Amy is awake."

Justin quickly put the cap on his pen and stood up. "Thanks."

Mounting the steps to the second floor, Dr. Morgan again wondered if his patient had remembered anything else that might help solve who she was and who the two young children were.

Softly he entered Room 212 to find Amy staring out the window at the mountains. She didn't move or turn her head as he came over, and even his quiet "good morning" brought no response. His brows drew together in a puzzled frown and he placed his fingers on her wrist, all the while watching her face. Still no movement came.

"Amy," Dr. Morgan placed a gentle hand on her shoulder.

With a sudden start, Amy's head jerked around and she lifted frightened eyes to the doctor, breathing rapidly. "Oh," she gasped, pressing a hand over her racing heart. "You startled me!"

"I'm sorry. That wasn't my intention," Justin's words were soothing and apologetic but his face held a slight look of concern. "I spoke to you, but you didn't answer. What were you thinking about?" Pulling up a chair, Dr. Morgan sat down.

Amy drew a deep breath and relaxed. "I'm not sure. I—" She paused and bit her lip.

Dr. Morgan waited silently. Was she remembering? He could only wait.

At last she began again in a half dreamy way. "I got them out of something . . . something dark, or . . . or bad or—I don't know. And then we had to hurry. I don't know why. But we had to keep moving, Danny, Jenny and I." Her words came quicker. "It got dark and I couldn't start a fire. I was scared." Unconsciously she had gripped the edge of her blanket and now held it clenched in her hands. She stared at the opposite wall as though watching on it bits of the past she was trying to recall.

She was clearly agitated and confused, yet Dr. Morgan hesitated about trying to stop her talking, for though she may stop speaking about it, he knew she would still be thinking. So he continued silent yet watchful; ready to quiet his patient should he need to but hoping and praying she would be all right.

"I don't know how long we walked but it felt like years. I was afraid. What was I afraid of?" She turned to look at her silent listener before continuing, giving him no time to answer. "They cried. Poor things. I knew we were going to die. I couldn't go on. Everything is blurred and I don't know if it was a dream or reality. Then, just when I couldn't go on anymore, I saw a light. I know I must have walked towards it, but I don't remember it. I heard a dog bark and then I was here. And," she added in a strangely calm voice, "I don't know another single thing about me. It's strange isn't it, to live a life and then start all over again? Doctor, tell me honestly," she gripped his hand

tightly, "will I ever remember again?" Her dark eyes seemed to be searching the young doctor's face for the truth.

Justin had no choice. "I don't know," he answered quietly. "You may, or you may not. For now, don't try. Focus on gaining your strength and getting well."

Her hand dropped from his and she lay still for several long minutes. "Doctor, I want to leave this place."

"This room?"

Amy's head nodded. "When can I go?"

"I expect you'll be out of here before Christmas," was the easy answer, spoken in light tones, though inwardly Justin was faced with a new problem. Where would this girl go when she was released from the hospital? She couldn't be left on her own, could she?

Almost as though reading his thoughts, Amy asked, "Where will I go when I leave? I don't know if I have a home."

"Let's cross that bridge when we come to it, shall we? We'll pray about it and God will show the way."

Amy looked up at him. "Do you pray?"

"Yes, I do."

Turning her face away without a word, Amy closed her eyes. She was tired.

"You did right about not pushing her, Morgan," Dr. Stern nodded his head. "Things like that can't be forced. I know it's difficult to wait and wonder about her and the little ones, but trying to force a mind to remember tends only to make it worse."

The two doctors were sitting in Dr. Morgan's office late that afternoon. Dr. Stern, coming home from a conference in a nearby town, had decided to stop by for a visit, and Justin was relieved to see him.

"It's not that I thought there was something else to do," he said. "It's just so baffling."

Smiling, the consulting physician replied, "The human mind has baffled many older men than you for centuries and, I suppose, always will. By the way, you are looking brighter and more awake than when I last saw you."

"I was kicked out of the hospital for the night and sent home."

Dr. Stern chuckled. "Not a bad idea. I'll remember that and try it on some of my colleagues. But I must be on my way. And, as always, don't hesitate to call if you want a second opinion."

"Thank you."

The two men shook hands and Dr. Stern departed, leaving Dr. Morgan sitting at his desk.

The days passed by. The first of winter's snows blanketed the mountains with a glistening covering of white; the air was cold, the wind biting. People tramped about in snowshoes, laughing and waiting for the snowplows to free the center of their small town. Farther up the mountain, in the Morgan cabin, Mr. Morgan and Adam set about shoveling snow while Sara, with a well bundled up Danny beside her, packed snow into a small snowman.

Back at the hospital, Amy was growing restless. She could now move about with crutches, and daily her desire to leave grew. She moved from room to room in silent impatience. Since her last talk with Dr. Morgan, she hadn't mentioned any of her memories, but there were times when she would lie in bed, or sit unmoving in her chair, staring at nothing. Such times would result in increased restlessness and Justin watched her with some anxiety.

Rebekah A. Morris

~ *6* ~

Standing in his office, Dr. Morgan looked out the window at the snow falling gently from a grey sky.

"How long are you going to keep her here?"

Dr. Morgan turned. His colleagues were grouped about his desk waiting. He shook his head. "I don't know. If she had someone to help her, I'd release her today, but she can't stay on her own, and since she hasn't remembered anything, well . . ." he paused. Moving back to his desk he sank into his chair with a sigh.

There was a silence in the office. The four doctors were somewhat baffled by this patient. Should she be released and allowed to try living on her own? Such a thought didn't seem advisable, and everyone racked their brains for a solution to the problem.

A knock sounded on the door.

"Come in," Dr. Morgan called.

The door opened and Intern Philips stepped in. He glanced at Wright, Hollend and Douglas and then looked at Dr. Morgan.

"Am I needed, Philips?"

"I'm not sure, sir," was the unexpected and somewhat hesitant reply. "It's Amy."

"Is she ill?" The words were quick and Dr. Morgan was all attention.

"No sir, but she saw her name on her chart and—" again he hesitated.

"Come on, Philips, what happened? Is she remembering?"

"She said her name wasn't Jones, it was Smith."

Surprised glances were flashed between the doctors gathered and then Dr. Morgan asked slowly, "Did she say anything else?"

Philips shook his head. "Not a word. And she said that as though she didn't know how the wrong name got on the paper."

Justin's mind was busy. Was anything coming back to this girl's memory? Perhaps something could be found out about her if this new name was really the correct one. Would she remember other things? These and a hundred other thoughts all rushed through the doctor's mind in a matter of seconds. Aloud he asked, "What is Amy doing now?"

"Nurse Franklin is with her."

"Good. She'll be all right for a little while then." Nurse Franklin was a friendly but very dedicated old nurse. When the new hospital was about to open, she had asked if she might work there. This was granted gladly, for she came highly recommended by Dr. Stern.

"Thank you, Philips."

The young intern nodded and slipped from the room, closing the door behind him.

"Why don't you see if Grace Franklin could take her home?" Dr. Hollend suggested.

Justin shook his head. "No, she has two grandchildren living with her and doesn't have time or

room for another person, much less one in Amy's condition."

Dr. Douglas spoke up, "I'd offer my home, but with three youngsters my wife is working too hard as it is. And our house is rather small."

A general chuckle went around the room, for Dr. Douglas lived in crackerjack house that was bursting at the seams. There was scarcely any room for a friendly visit.

"Well, it seems to me," Dr. Wright leaned back in his chair, "that the only logical place for Amy to go would be where there is plenty of room, people who could help her, young ones who might wake memories and where her doctor goes quite often anyway."

"My parents' house?"

"Why not?"

"Of course she can come here, Justin," Mrs. Morgan exclaimed. "Why didn't we think of it sooner. We have plenty of room and perhaps being with Danny and Jenny would awaken her forgotten memories."

The family was seated around the blazing open fire in the Morgan living room as they had been on that night over two months ago. The youngsters had been in bed for half an hour and now the older members were discussing Dr. Wright's suggestion.

Justin turned to his father. "Dad, what do you think?"

Mr. Morgan nodded. "I agree with your mother. I think it would be a good idea. It is something I have thought of more than once but always wondered if perhaps her memory would come back before she was ready to leave the hospital."

"Can she come tomorrow, Just?" Sara questioned. "Which room should we give her, Mother? Should she be going up and down the stairs much?"

Justin threw a pillow at her. "Hang on a second, Sara; you can plan where she's staying later. But no, she shouldn't be going up and down the stairs much. At least not yet. Give her a room downstairs. Adam," he turned to his brother who had been quiet throughout the entire discussion, "What do you think of this?"

"If we can help her, I don't see why she shouldn't come," the reply was quiet and Adam's face was sober. He was the most thoughtful and quiet of all the Morgan children. "Since God brought her to our door, it seems as though He wants us to help her."

A silence fell over the group sitting in the flickering glow of the firelight. Adam's words had reminded them all that Amy's coming had not been a mere accident. Why she had come and who she was, remained a mystery, but she was here and in need of a home.

Mr. Morgan at last broke the silence. "Let her come as soon as you wish, Son."

"Thank you." The words were simple but the tone expressed great relief.

A log broke in two sending a shower of sparks up the chimney, and the old clock on the mantle began striking the hour of ten in deep, slow tones.

Justin rose. "I must go. I didn't realize it was so late. If all goes well, I'll release Amy tomorrow and bring her up."

The others rose also and followed him into the entryway where he put on his coat.

"Thanks again for letting her come here. I don't know if it will help her memory any to be around the little ones,

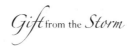

but she couldn't remain at the hospital much longer."

"Be careful driving down, Justin."

"I will, Mother. And," he added, kissing her, "I'll call when I reach the hospital. Good night."

It was a matter of seconds after Justin replaced the phone in his office when Philips appeared at the door.

"I'm glad you are back, sir."

Dr. Morgan looked up in surprise. "What's wrong?"

"I'm not sure anything is really wrong, but Amy won't go to bed. She is restless and hasn't eaten. She won't talk, but she doesn't have a fever."

"Who is with her?" Quickly Dr. Morgan was getting ready.

"Nurse Jones."

"How long has she been this way?"

Philips glanced at his watch. "I went up to check when her tray came down untouched at seven-twenty-five."

Justin glanced at his watch. It was nearly ten-thirty now. "Why wasn't I called?"

"No one thought it was anything to worry about, sir. Dr. Wright and Dr. Douglas didn't want to bother you since there really was no cause for alarm." The young intern spoke apologetically and looked worried.

Seeing this, Justin hastened to reassure him. "It probably isn't anything to worry about. She's been restless for several days now. I'll run up and see if I can't get her to sleep. Thanks for filling in for me, Philips." And Dr. Morgan hurried away.

On the stairs, Dr. Douglas met him. "Going up to check on Amy?"

Justin nodded. "Why didn't anyone call me?"

"And tell you what? A missed meal should not be alarming; as for not going to bed, that's only been in the last hour, and we figured you'd be back. Calm down, Morgan." He placed a restraining hand on his colleague's arm. "Nurse Jones hasn't called for anyone, so things can't be too serious."

Drawing a deep breath, Dr. Morgan gave a slight smile. "I was rather startled by the news. Perhaps it will help if I tell her she's leaving the hospital tomorrow."

"It might at that. Things worked out?"

Dr. Morgan nodded and the two physicians parted.

Pausing outside Room 212, Dr. Morgan knocked softly and a moment later Nurse Jones opened the door. She looked visibly relieved and held open the door.

"Hello, Amy."

Amy stood at the window with her back to the door and didn't turn around, though she acknowledged the greeting with a grunt.

Shaking her head, Nurse Jones murmured, "She's been like this since I've been here. Won't talk, won't sit, won't sleep."

Dr. Morgan nodded and stepped farther into the room. "Amy, I was planning on releasing you from the hospital tomorrow and sending you up to stay with Danny and Jenny, but if you don't get to bed and get some rest, I'll have to keep you another day or so."

Turning around, Amy looked at him, her face full of questions, fear and frustration. "You really will let me leave tomorrow?" she asked.

"If you take your medicine and get to bed now."

"It won't do any good," she muttered half aloud.

Dr. Morgan eyed her searchingly. "Why?"

"I can't sleep."

"You haven't tried."

"I tried earlier." She hobbled over to the bed and sat down. "But I can't remember the song and it's driving me crazy!" Her words were frantic.

"Do you know any of the tune?" The question was quiet and calming.

"Only parts."

"Hum them for me."

With her eyes on the floor, Amy hummed a phrase or two and then waited. She wasn't sure Dr. Morgan could help her remember the song, but it was worth a try.

Dr. Morgan had no need for any song book to remember that tune, and he sang the first verse softly.

"God that madest earth and heaven,
Darkness and light,
Who the day for toil has given
For rest the night . . ."

"That's it! Why was I remembering that song?" Amy demanded as the nurse came and helped her into bed, settled her pillows and gave her her medicine.

"I'm not sure," Dr. Morgan replied, "but perhaps it is because my sister sang it to you several times just before your fever broke."

Amy was quiet as Justin looked at her chart and then moved to the door.

"Doctor," she called to him just as he snapped off the light. "Please, won't you sing the entire song. I don't know why it was bothering me, but I want to hear it all."

For answer, Dr. Morgan began the evening hymn

once again standing in the doorway. He sang it with feeling, remembering that night when Heather had sung it. He prayed it would calm Amy now as it had then, but he didn't know that down the hall another patient, hearing the haunting tune, relaxed and slept, or that Dr. Wright and Dr. Douglas paused on the stairs to listen, while the few nurses stood silently at their posts letting the music refresh them for the long, quiet night ahead.

The song over, Dr. Morgan shut Amy's door and moved quietly down the hall to the stairs. He glanced curiously at his fellow physicians standing on the stairs, passed them and headed towards his office.

He checked his desk for anything important, put on his boots, grabbed his coat and headed to his small boarding house down the street, little dreaming what comfort and rest that song had given.

"Oh, I'm tired," he yawned, taking off his boots and hanging his coat on its hook. "At least Amy will have a good home, and maybe I won't worry so much about her." He sighed, snapped off his light and crawled into bed.

The sun was shining from an icy blue sky when Justin came into the hospital lobby. He knew the sun would melt the top layer of the snow before it sank in the west, leaving ice everywhere.

"Good morning, Dr. Morgan," Dr. Wright greeted him. "It sure will be a fine morning to drive up the mountain, but," he shook his head. "I'm not sure I'd want to drive down it this evening."

Justin laughed. "That's why I'm coming down right after lunch."

"What! Not staying to perhaps become snowed in and forced to take a vacation?"

"I wouldn't dream of leaving you to handle the hundreds of patients alone," Justin retorted.

Both men laughed, shook hands and went on their way.

The drive with Amy up to the Morgan cabin was slow but uneventful. Dr. Morgan drove carefully but at the same time kept an eye on the girl beside him. He hoped and prayed that living with a family would help her gain strength and perhaps even her memory. Would Danny know who she was when they arrived? It had been a long time since he had seen her.

Sitting silently, Amy watched the snowy landscape move past the windows of the truck. She squinted at the brightness caused by the sun, but spoke not a word. Her thoughts were a puzzling mixture of unanswered questions. Who was she and where had she come from? Why did she remember nothing? Would the two children she had gotten to safety bring any memories back? She was nervous and began fiddling with the buttons on her coat. What would these people be like? What if she didn't like it up here? How could she leave with all this snow?

~ 7 ~

"Hey." A calm voice made her turn and look at the driver.

Dr. Morgan glanced briefly at her and placed a gloved hand over her restless one. "Relax," he told her, "everything is going to be all right. Stop fretting about what you can't remember. Live in the here and now, not the past. There," he pointed ahead "you can see the house up beyond those trees."

Smoke was curling heavenward in a friendly fashion from the stone chimney that rose from the snow covered roof. The truck rounded another bend and the whole front of the house could be seen; the dark logs looking warm and snug against the backdrop of winter's white blanket. Curtains hanging in the many windows, the porch swept clean of snow and the shoveled path all spoke silently of being such a happy, lived in house, that Amy could only gaze through a film of unshed tears.

A dog barked as Justin shut off the motor, and a collie came bounding from behind the house, tail wagging, to leap up on him as he got out of the truck.

"Whoa, Captain!" Justin staggered back a step and then roughed up the dog's fur before he pushed him down. "I'm glad to see you too, old boy. Now," he continued as he carefully made his way to the other side of the truck, "no jumping on Amy. She's not strong enough to withstand your assaults."

The dog whined and barked, pranced around and barked some more. His barking had its affect for the front door of the house opened and several people in coats came out on the porch. One of them whistled for the dog and then called to Justin, "You need any help?"

"No thanks," Justin called back, carefully helping Amy from the truck and then, after he had shut the door, lifting her and carrying her inside, where he set her down in a chair beside the crackling fire.

Mrs. Morgan quickly divested Amy of her coat, scarf and gloves, introducing herself as she did so.

"Welcome to our cabin, Amy," Mr. Morgan greeted her with a smile. He had already met her several times at the hospital when he was in town at his office.

Amy smiled almost timidly back and let her gaze wander around the large open room. She liked what she saw:, the picture window looking out over the blinding whiteness, the baby grand piano, the fire, the cozy arrangement of the furniture. Unconsciously she gave a sigh and relaxed into the comfortable chair.

"Amy," Dr. Morgan's voice caused her to look up. A young man was standing beside him. "I'd like you to meet Adam, my younger brother, and the only one I've got."

Hardly had this introduction been given when another voice was heard and Dr. Morgan turned to call, "Sare, bring them over here."

Coming at once, Sara carried Jenny on her hip while Danny trotted along behind her.

"Hi!" Sara greeted Amy as though she had seen her a few days ago. "I'm glad Just finally let us keep you for a while. I don't think it was fair for the hospital to have you

for as long as they did. I'm the one who needs another girl around here." She kept up a bright chatter to cover the silence, sensing that Amy wasn't hearing much, for her eyes were on the little ones.

Jenny, wanting to get down and practice her crawling, squirmed and wiggled until Sara set her on the floor. For a moment Danny just stood and looked at Amy, and Amy gazed back. Each seemed trying to place the other in their memory. At last Danny turned and wandered off without a word.

"Justin," Mrs. Morgan turned to her eldest son, "you are staying for lunch, aren't you?"

Justin glanced at his watch, "Sure, but I can't stay too late unless I want to slide down the mountain."

"You'd end up in your own hospital," Adam laughed and then the two brothers left the room.

Mr. and Mrs. Morgan, seeing Sara drop into a chair across the fire from Amy, slipped from the room as well, leaving them together with the little ones. They knew Sara would be good company.

"Good bye, Amy," Dr. Morgan said, stopping beside the couch where she was resting after having eaten lunch with the others at the table. "Take it easy with that leg. You're in good hands here." He smiled and pressed her hand gently.

Amy said a quiet good bye and then, sitting up, she watched silently out the large windows as moments later the doctor's pickup truck left the house heading back towards the village, down the mountain to the hospital and everything Amy could clearly remember, leaving her behind, alone with comparative strangers. Suddenly she felt an intense loneliness steal across her and she blinked back the tears which would come and trickle down her cheeks in spite of herself.

A cheerful whistling caused her to quickly wipe her eyes and lie back on the pillows as Adam entered the room with a few books. If he noticed the traces of tears he didn't say anything, but he set the books on a stool beside her.

"Should you grow tired of doing nothing, here are a few books you can read if you want."

"Where are the . . . others?" She hesitated, wondering what to call Mr. and Mrs. Morgan.

Adam answered easily as he stepped across the room to put new logs on the fire. "Dad's in his study, Sara is putting the little ones down for naps and," he brushed the hearth with the brush, "I'm not sure where Mother is." He stood up, looking down at the fire which was now blazing comfortably, dusted his hands on his pants and said casually, "Well, I've got to get more wood. Be back soon."

With that he was gone and Amy was left to herself.

Picking up the first book, Amy opened it and began to read. If Adam's idea when he brought the books was to help Amy not think, it worked, for she was so lost in the story when he came with an armload of logs to add to the wood box, that she didn't so much as glance over at him.

The afternoon passed by with Amy scarcely noticing, for after reading for a while, Sara came in and talked until the little ones were up from their naps. When Mrs. Morgan came to say that supper was ready, Amy looked surprised. Never had an afternoon in the hospital passed so quickly.

The evening, with the entire family gathered in the large living room around the blazing fire, talking and laughing together, was delightful to the newcomer who lay on the couch in silence taking it all in. This was something new, something that didn't awaken any dim feelings of almost knowing yet not quite.

"Sara," Mr. Morgan spoke during a lull in the conversation, "it is growing late. Will you play our evening hymns for us?"

Sara nodded and, rising from her chair, handed Jenny to Adam before sliding onto the bench before the baby grand which Amy had admired.

Everyone was rising and Amy wondered if she was expected to do the same.

"Don't try to stand with the rest of us tonight, Dear," Mrs. Morgan said quietly as Amy half rose. "We'll bring you the hymn book if you want it, or you can just listen tonight."

"May I just listen?" queried Amy, not feeling sure she could sing.

"Of course."

The couch was moved somewhat so Amy could look at the others. It made a lovely picture, everyone standing about the piano. Mr. Morgan, tall and broad shouldered with a little grey in his dark hair, holding Danny who had one arm wrapped lovingly about his neck. Beside them stood Mrs. Morgan. Such a look of peaceful sweetness was on her face that it was some time before Amy was aware of anything or anyone else. Adam, she noticed, pulling her eyes from Mrs. Morgan, was taller than his father, with lighter hair and the build of someone who had spent years outside in the elements. He was bending over, attempting to help straighten the sheet music for Sara who sat on the piano bench, but he was not having much success, for Jenny, who he was holding in one arm, kept grabbing

Sara's hair in a tight baby grasp.

Giving an involuntary smile, Amy turned her head to gaze again at the flickering flames dancing in the fireplace. There was something comforting yet at the same time half frightening about those tongues of fire and the glowing logs. What was it? She wanted to turn her eyes away, but they seemed held, fastened by an irresistible pull that she couldn't break, locked on a memory which she couldn't quite recall. A tightness crept about her throat, a shiver ran down her spine, her hands clenched; she couldn't breathe! She had to get away!

~ 8 ~

It was only when the tender melodies of the evening hymns softly filled the room that the tightness faded away, the shivers ceased, her hands relaxed, and as the menacing flames, under the influence of the quieting words being sung, returned once more into a cozy fire, she drew a deep breath and lay back, exhausted.

When the last hymn was sung, the notes dying in the quiet room, Mr. Morgan offered up a prayer, not forgetting the newest addition to the household. Amy listened while a few tears trickled down her cheeks. She couldn't remember anyone praying for her before. Quiet good nights were said and Sara and Adam, taking the little ones, disappeared from the room, and moments later Amy noticed them crossing the walkway up above.

"Amy," Mrs. Morgan asked gently, coming over to the couch. "Do you think you feel up to walking a little ways to your bedroom? Or shall Mr. Morgan carry you?"

"I . . . I think I can make it," Amy replied almost timidly. She had wondered where she would sleep. With the gentle help of Mrs. Morgan, Amy limped from the room, down a short hall and into a small but pleasant room. A lamp was glowing on the rustic table beside the bed. The room itself was papered in a light blue print while the quilt on the bed was a deep blue. A chest of drawers stood beside a closet door and a chair was in a position to enjoy a charming view from the window when the curtains were opened.

A few moments later, Amy lay between the white sheets with warm blankets pulled over her.

"Good night, Dear," Mrs. Morgan said softly, turning out the light. "God give you sweet dreams."

In the dark, Amy drew a deep breath and relaxed. The room had a home smell to it, not a sterile hospital smell. Slipping one hand to the top of her covers, she reached out and felt again the soft fabric of the quilt. "And it's blue,' she whispered to herself with a smile. Noticing a faint light, Amy turned her head and saw a tiny crack in the curtains. "Moonlight. I wonder if it's full." That was the last conscious thought Amy had before falling into a deep, peaceful sleep.

Sitting in his small room in his boarding house in town, Justin replaced the phone and sighed. He couldn't get Amy out of his mind. His father's call had relieved his mind somewhat, but still he wondered.

"Dad thought she looked a bit frightened before they started singing," Justin mused. "He didn't know if it was the fire or the thought of the singing, but after the songs started she relaxed. What a puzzle! How can we trace someone whose name is as common as hers is? Fire? Singing? What was she doing in the mountains to begin with?" Sighing again in frustration at the multitude of questions that were now racing through his brain, Justin sprang up and began to pace his limited floor space. "What if she wakes up during the night?" Realizing for the first time that should Amy awaken during the night there would be no nurse to answer her call, Justin halted beside his small desk.

A quick phone call up to the Morgan cabin reassured him that Amy would be checked on several times during the night.

"Relax, Son," Mr. Morgan told him. "Your mother and I have had sick people in the house before. I think we can handle one who can't remember. She was quite tired, and I think she'll sleep through the night just fine."

"You'll call if anything happens, right?"

A chuckle came over the phone line. "Justin Morgan, quit fussing. You know we'll call you. Now get some rest and let us do the same."

"Sorry, Dad. It's just—"

"I know, but we can talk tomorrow, all right?"

"Okay. Good-night."

For several long minutes Justin remained standing with his hand on the phone.

"There's got to be some way we can find something out." He resumed his pacing. "It's as though we had a puzzle without all the pieces. No, we have all the pieces only they are locked up where no one can get at them. I wonder if we'll ever know who they are and why they came.

Something Adam had said before came back to his mind. "Since God brought them to our house, it must have been for a reason."

Somehow the thought calmed him and sent him to his knees where he spent a long time praying, for Amy, for himself and his family as they sought to help her, for Danny and Jenny, and also for whatever families were somewhere searching for their missing loved ones.

A faint light was coming into the room when Amy opened her eyes. For a moment she couldn't figure out where she was. A feeling of panic began to well up inside of her until she heard a dog barking and smelled the delicious smell of pancakes.

Fifteen minutes later she slowly limped her way down the hall and into the dining room. Sara was busy feeding Jenny while Danny shoveled bites of pancakes into his mouth as fast as he could, hardly taking time to chew.

"You'll choke, Danny. Slow down," Amy admonished with a smile.

Sara looked up. "Good morning. How did you sleep? Mother, Amy's here for breakfast!" She called the last over her shoulder to the kitchen.

Sitting down and leaning her crutch against another chair, Amy looked out the large windows towards the mountain top and saw snowflakes falling gently. "I slept fine. That snow . . ."

"It's pretty, isn't it?" Sara turned and looked out until Jenny demanded another bite.

"There's so much. Do you ever get tired of it?"

Laughing, Sara offered Jenny a drink before replying. "Before spring comes I'm ready to move down south."

Just then Mrs. Morgan entered the room with a plate of hot pancakes, crisp bacon and two steaming fried eggs. "Good morning, Amy. I hope you are hungry." Setting the plate down before Amy, she poured a glass of milk from a metal pitcher on the table, set it next to the plate and sat down nearby.

Amy's eyes were wide as she stared at her plate of food. "I . . . I'm hungry, but I don't think I can eat that much!"

Mrs. Morgan smiled and patted her hand. "Justin told me to fatten you up, so I'm trying my best. Just eat what you can. You may be hungrier than you think." She placed the maple syrup before Amy and rose. "Danny, where did all your food go?"

Danny, his face covered with sticky syrup, grinned and his eyes crinkled. With sticky fingers he pointed down his shirt as he replied, "Down there."

"In your shirt?"

"No, my tummy."

Soon Danny was cleaned up and trotted off to go find Adam. Amy began eating. Everything tasted as delicious as it had smelled and with Sara's bright conversation, Jenny's entertaining baby antics and Mrs. Morgan bustling about, it was a great surprise to Amy when she realized that her plate was nearly empty. "I suppose I was hungry," she said.

Limping into the front room, Amy sank onto the couch and looked about her. It was such a large, cheery room, yet there was a feeling of coziness about it too that was appealing on such a cold, snowy day.

"Grandpa's coming!" Danny's excited voice at the window caused Amy to turn with a start. She saw Mr. Morgan and Adam coming towards the house carrying snow shovels. Upon noticing the two little faces pressed against the window, for Jenny had crawled over and pulled herself up beside Danny, the men stopped and waved, and then Adam tossed a few lightly packed snowballs against the window causing a squeal of delight from Jenny and giggles from Danny.

Suddenly Amy's throat contracted and a rush of tears filled her eyes. A momentary picture had flashed through her mind but before she could quite recall it, it had vanished. She was silent as the two men entered the living room moments later.

"Well, good morning Amy," Mr. Morgan greeted his new guest with a smile as he approached the couch. "How did you sleep last night?" Then his face grew sympathetic. "Is something wrong?" He had noticed the unshed tears.

Amy looked up with a small smile. "No," she said, but her look contradicted her words. "I think I just remembered something but now I don't know what it was."

"My advice to you, young lady," Mr. Morgan replied with a kind smile, "is not to try to think of anything right now, but I feel that's like telling Justin not to fret over his patients." His voice dropped to a confidential whisper as he added, "It doesn't work, you know. He frets over them anyhow."

This time a real smile turned up the corners of Amy's mouth.

"Now, how did you sleep?"

"Better than I have for a long time, I think. I don't really remember much of anything until this morning."

"Good. Maybe that will make Justin stop fretting over you." Turning to Sara who had just come in the room, he asked, "Has your brother called again?"

Sara shook her head. "Not since you left."

Right at that moment the telephone rang loudly. Stepping through the space which separated dining room from living room, Mr. Morgan picked up the receiver. "Hello . . . Yes, Justin, she's up and says she's slept better than she has for a long time. That's not saying much for your hospital, you know. . . ." He whispered something to his wife and then said aloud, "Yes, she ate a good breakfast. . . . No, I haven't had a chance. Just got in from clearing the

drive. . . . Sure I'll be in town. . . . Yep. . . . All right. Bye."
Replacing the receiver, Mr. Morgan turned. "How
many times a day do you think that boy will be calling us?"

"At least a dozen," Sara laughed, lightly running her
fingers up and down a few scales on the piano. "I
sometimes wonder what he'd do with thirty patients. What
do you think Justin would be like with that many patients,
Adam?" She paused in her playing to listen to his reply as
he stirred the fire and added a few more logs.

"He'd settle down and be just fine," was the quiet
answer.

"Humph," Sara snorted, as though not quite sure she
agreed. Then her fingers dashed off into a lively version of
"Jingle Bells."

"Sara!" Adam groaned, "it's not Christmas yet!"

"Who said 'Jingle Bells' was a Christmas song?" Sara
retorted merrily. "There's snow on the ground, isn't there?"

Amy, settled on the couch, watched and listened to
the exchange between Adam and Sara in silence. When
Adam, standing up, had remarked to her in low tones, "I
hope her songs don't drive you crazy," Amy had only
smiled. She didn't think any song would bother her.

Picking up the book she had been reading the day
before, Amy opened it and began reading, while Sara, her
mood seeming to wear off, settled into steady practice, and
for some time the only sound heard in the room was the
lovely notes of the piano.

The morning passed by before Amy was quite aware
of it, and after lunch Mrs. Morgan suggested she lie down
and rest for a while. "The little ones will be taking naps and
you look tired. We don't want Justin saying we didn't take

good care of you."

"All right," Amy agreed readily. "I am tired." She paused a moment before the dining room windows and looked out over the snow. "That's what I feel my mind is like," she said quietly as though to herself. "A large blank nothing. Only the snow sparkles when the sun shines, but my mind doesn't. It's just empty."

Coming into the dining room just then, Adam caught the girl's troubled words. "The best thing to do with an empty mind is to fill it with good things." His words were quiet and he continued his way into the kitchen.

Amy turned to look after him. "Fill it with good things," she murmured thoughtfully, limping from the room and down the hall into her lovely little room. "I wonder what he meant?"

~*9*~

In town Dr. Justin Morgan was sitting in his office fiddling with his pen. "Maybe I should go up and see how she is this afternoon." He looked across his desk to see his father shaking his head. "You don't think I should?" he asked.

"No, I don't," Mr. Morgan replied honestly. "And I'll tell you why. First, Amy's hardly had time to settle in, and if she feels that you are going to constantly check in on her, she's not going to be able to relax and be herself.

"Second, I think that Adam and Sara are good for Amy right now in their own ways. Let them have a chance to see what they can do without you constantly interfering.

"Third," and Mr. Morgan smiled, "if you keep coming up to the house, your colleagues might decide you can't handle a hospital without running home every day to talk to your parents."

"What? Is Justin talking about running away again?" Dr. Wright knocked lightly on the open door and stepped inside. "First he won't leave the hospital and now all he wants to do is run away. I say Mr. Morgan, you should have taught your son some responsibility."

Mr. Morgan laughed with Dr. Wright as he stood to

shake hands with him. "I'm just trying to convince him to stick around here for a time and see if he won't like it."

"If he'd give himself half a chance," Dr. Wright grinned, "he might find he wants to become a doctor after all."

Leaning back in his chair, Justin just shook his head with a smile. It had been a slow morning at the hospital, which had given him plenty of time to wonder about Amy and time to talk with his father.

Before anything else could be said, Philips burst into the office. "Dr. Morgan, Dr. Wright, we just got a call. There's been a skiing accident at the lodge and it sounds pretty bad. There could be half a dozen victims brought in!"

Instantly Dr. Morgan was on his feet fully alert and ready for action. "Wright, you'd better see that the operating team is standing by. Philips, alert Dr. Hollend and Dr. Douglas. You'll probably have to call Douglas, as I think he's already left. I'll make sure Mr. Thatcher is ready for x-rays."

Dr. Wright was already out the door before Dr. Morgan had finished speaking, and Philips hardly waited for the end before he too disappeared. Just before Dr. Morgan left his office, he remembered his father and turned. "Thanks for coming by, Dad. I'll probably get up there in a day or two. Call me about anything. Sorry, I've got to rush." He held out his hand.

Mr. Morgan gave it a quick, firm grip and said, "We will, but don't worry if we don't call every day. Now get ready to help your next patients."

The rest of the day was a whirlwind of activity in the small town hospital. The skiing accident had brought over

a dozen injured persons to the hospital for treatment
though several were only minor injuries and could be sent
home soon after. It wasn't until late that night that Dr.
Morgan found himself standing in the front lobby with Dr.
Douglas.

"We haven't had this many patients brought in on
one day the entire time the hospital's been open," Dr.
Douglas remarked, rubbing the back of his neck."

"That's for sure. Well, I think Hollend, Wright and I
can handle them for the night. You can head home. We'll
call you if you're needed."

"If who's needed?" Dr. Wright asked, sinking down
into one of the chairs. He looked tired. Never before had he
handled so many surgeries in an afternoon as the chief
surgeon.

Justin smiled. "I was just telling Douglas that he
could go home for the night. You, Hollend and I will take
over here."

Dr. Wright nodded. "We can handle it."

"Good," Justin said "Then get your coat and get out
of here, Douglas." Dr. Douglas was standing in a daze
before the door. He'd been on duty the night before and
hadn't had a chance to catch even forty winks before
Philip's call had brought him back to the hospital.

As Dr. Morgan sat in his office, having checked the
patients and offered to take the first shift with Wright so
Hollend could get some sleep, his mind went over each
patient and their injuries. "Only one concussion," he
mused, "but enough broken bones and other injuries. And
then there's Lincoln Kern with that back injury. I'm glad
we were able to get him transported to Jackson today. I

think I'll call Dr. Stern in the morning and check on him, though."

The thought of the hospital's consulting physician brought Amy back to his mind and again he wondered if her memory would ever come back. "I wonder if it's a physical block that is causing her condition or a mental one. Could it be that there is something, or perhaps more than one thing, in her past which is so disturbing that her mind is blocking it? If that is the case, what is it going to take to remove that block?" For some time he sat unmoving, his brain busy analyzing every angle and detail that he could think of or remember about his interaction with the unknown girl.

"Dr. Morgan?"

Justin's thoughts quickly returned and he sat up. "Yes?"

One of the nurses was standing in the doorway. "Mrs. Brewer is in a lot of pain and very restless, sir. Her temperature is up and her pulse rate is fast."

Dr. Morgan stood up at once. "I'll come right now. How are the others? Do you know?"

The nurse shook her head. "I haven't heard anything, sir, and I was on duty in the hall."

"All right." He glanced down at his watch in the dim light of the stairs. "It's about time I made my rounds anyway. I'll first see to Mrs. Brewer."

Amy had retired that night with a feeling of . . . well, she couldn't quite find a name for it. It was family, peace, security and love all mixed up somehow in the large house in the snow. As she lay awake under the blankets and the blue quilt, she stared through a crack in the curtains at the moon. "I wish I could stay here forever," she thought. "At least, I think I do. Where did I come from and why can't I remember anything? What was it Adam said? Fill an empty mind with good things?" What good things could she fill it with if she couldn't remember anything? Suddenly part of a verse from one of the evening hymns floated through her mind.

"Earth's joys grow dim; its glories pass away.
Change and decay in all around I see;
O Thou who changest not, abide with me."

Then another phrase:
"Thro' clouds and sunshine, oh abide with me!"

Perhaps that was what Adam was thinking about. "Thro' clouds and sunshine," she mused. "I feel like I'm in a cloud or maybe a fog. Abide with me. I wonder what I thought about prayer before—well, before all this happened. Dr. Morgan says he believes in prayer, and his father sounds like he believes in it. I suspect Mrs. Morgan and Sara believe in it too. What do I believe? Oh!" she turned restlessly. "Why can't I remember anything?"

For some time it seemed that no matter which direction Amy tried to turn her thoughts, she always ended up with the same cry, "Why can't I remember?" At last she fell asleep, determined to ask Adam about what he meant in the morning.

A snowstorm was blowing down across the mountains when Amy awoke the following day. She felt tired and wondered at first if she should just remain in bed, but at last, feeling that doing anything was preferable to remaining alone, she rose.

It was later than the previous morning, and breakfast had been eaten by the rest of the family when Amy at last entered the dining room where Mrs. Morgan was seated. Mrs. Morgan rose with a smile. "Good morning, Amy. You just have a seat and I'll have breakfast ready for you in no time."

"I'm not very hungry," Amy said, sinking down onto a chair.

"That's what you said yesterday, Dear," Mrs. Morgan laughed. "We'll just see if you can't put away another hearty breakfast."

With a sigh Amy leaned her chin on her hand, her elbow resting on the table as she stared out at the swirling, blowing snow.

"Good morning." The quiet greeting startled Amy, and she turned to see Adam coming from the front room. "It sure is snowing outside."

Here was her chance, Amy decided, and she blurted out, "What good things do I fill it with?"

Adam didn't have to ask what she was talking about, but simply replied, "Whatsoever things are true, whatsoever things are honest, whatsoever things are just, whatsoever things are pure, whatsoever things are lovely, whatsoever things are of good report; if there be any virtue, and if there be any praise, think on these things." Adam quoted the words in his quiet manner and added, "Fill your mind with those things and the rest will take care of itself."

Amy didn't reply, and Adam, picking up what he had come after, returned to the other room. Thoughtfully Amy ate her breakfast, not noticing what she ate or the somewhat troubled glances Mrs. Morgan sent her way.

Into the quiet dining room came Sara's eager voice, "Mother, Dad brought the boxes down!"

Smiling, Mrs. Morgan called back, "Wait a few more minutes, Sara, and let Amy finish her breakfast." Then, turning to her young guest, she added, "We're going to decorate today, except for the tree, and Sara is about as impatient at nineteen as she used to be at nine."

"Decorate?"

"For Christmas. You can help too, if you promise you won't wear yourself out."

When Mrs. Morgan and Amy entered the living room ten minutes later, they discovered the rest of the family waiting for them. The bustle and activity which followed was something Amy never forgot. Soon she found herself settled in a chair untangling Christmas tree lights while she watched the others unpack ornaments, bows and garlands. Every little while Sara would sit down before the piano and dash off a few bars of a Christmas carol which set everyone to singing. Even Danny and Jenny were not forgotten, and Jenny happily stood by a chair or a table, hanging on to a string of jingle bells and giggling every time she shook them, while Danny followed Adam and Mr. Morgan around, cheerfully getting in their way and not caring in the least if he was nearly stepped on numerous times. Sitting there watching the excitement, Amy wondered what it would have been like to have grown up in a family as happy and pleasant as this one must have been. Reaching the end of her string of lights, she leaned back in the chair, content to watch and listen.

Everyone was so busy that day that Amy had no time to sit and wonder about her life, and when she went to bed that night, her mind was so full of the pleasant things of the day that the troublesome thoughts of the previous night were forgotten.

The following day was much the same and Amy, feeling stronger and a little more sure of herself, asked to be allowed to help with supper. Mrs. Morgan accepted her offer with a smile.

To Amy it was a new experience. She had no knowledge of how to do anything, but, once Mrs. Morgan showed her how to peel the potatoes, Amy felt as though she must have done the same things before, for her hands moved with the speed and ease of someone quite used to the task. "It's strange, isn't it," she remarked thoughtfully. "I couldn't have told you how to peel a potato but now that I'm doing it, I feel as though I've done it many times, only I don't know where or when."

Mrs. Morgan nodded sympathetically, but said not a word.

When the potatoes were bubbling in the water, Amy gathered plates, glasses, napkins and silverware in preparation for setting the table. Humming a Christmas carol, she carried the items to the table and then stopped short. A sudden feeling of panic and confusion swept over her and she cried out, "I can't do it!"

~ *10* ~

Limping quickly from the dining room, while tears ran down her cheeks, the troubled girl fled to her room where she collapsed onto her bed and sobbed. Up until that time her forgotten memory had been troubling, but now she felt helpless and alone.

Back in the kitchen, Mrs. Morgan had heard the cry and hurried into the dining room only to find Amy gone. A quick glance at the unset table, and Mrs. Morgan was sure of what had happened. Stepping into the front room where the rest of the family were gathered, she said, "Adam, Sara, will you please finish supper and see that the table gets set?"

It was obvious that all had seen Amy's distress, for Mr. Morgan, Sara and Adam all looked troubled. "Of course, Mother," Adam replied quietly, standing up to take the spoon from his mother's hand. "Come on, Sara."

With many anxious glances down the hall after her mother, Sara slowly followed her brother into the dining room, after setting Jenny on the couch to read stories with Danny.

Pausing in the open doorway of Amy's room, Mrs. Morgan looked with tender eyes at the sobbing girl on the bed. She was so young and looked so helpless at that moment. "Amy," she said softly, stepping in and sitting on the edge of the bed.

Amy, on hearing her name spoken and feeling the gentle touch of a hand, wailed, "Why can't I remember?"

"I don't know, Child," Mrs. Morgan answered softly. "I don't know." Tenderly she stroked the light hair, praying inwardly for wisdom and comfort for this girl with only a name. Unconsciously she began humming one of the evening hymns. It was the tune Heather had first sung to Amy weeks before and the melody soothed her now as it did then. Gradually her sobs lessened and she lay quiet and still. So still was she that Mrs. Morgan wondered if she had fallen asleep, but when she rose and began to spread a blanket over her, Amy stirred.

"I'm not asleep," she said, her voice muffled by the pillow.

"Are you going to come eat now? Supper is probably about ready."

"I don't feel hungry," was the whispered reply.

Mrs. Morgan patted her shoulder. "All right, Dear. Come when you are ready. And remember this, we want you."

There was no reply, and Mrs. Morgan left the room wondering if she had done all she could.

Supper was nearly over when Amy appeared. Traces of tears were still on her face, but no one said a word as Adam, rising with his customary good manners, pulled out her chair for her. She didn't eat much and scarcely said a word all evening. When it was time for the evening hymns, she remained sitting in her chair and listened, a troubled look on her face.

After the little ones and Amy had gone to bed, the rest of the Morgan family remained sitting around the fire.

"What are we going to tell Justin when he calls?" Sara asked softly. "He hasn't called all day so I expect he'll be calling any time now."

Mrs. Morgan sighed and looked across at her husband. "I don't know. Perhaps he should come up and see her."

"What upset her this evening?" Mr. Morgan asked.

"She didn't know how to set the table, and I think it was the last straw. Her only cry when I went to her was 'why can't I remember?' I wanted to cry myself."

Just then the phone rang and Mr. Morgan rose quickly to answer it. "Hello. We were wondering when you'd get around to calling. . . . I see. Well, . . . no, she went to bed with the little ones tonight. . . . Justin, let me switch phones. It'll be easier to talk in the office. I'll put your mother on while I head there."

On hearing this, Mrs. Morgan rose and took the phone her husband handed her. "Hello, Son. Was the hospital busy today? . . . Oh, I see. . . . Yes, we decorated yesterday during the storm. . . . She was just fine, but there's Dad. Good-bye. . . . I love you too."

Returning to the front room, Mrs. Morgan settled herself once more in her chair. The room was quiet save for the soft sounds of the fire and the low murmur of Mr. Morgan's deep voice in the office.

Sara, curled up in one corner of the couch, frowned over at Adam as he absentmindedly straightened the fringe on the rug. "Why do you think she was fine yesterday, Mother, but tonight—" she didn't finish, but looked at her mother with a puzzled face.

"I don't know for sure. It could be that we kept her too busy yesterday to try to think and tonight, well, tonight she tried doing something alone for the first time since she's been sick and found out she didn't know how."

"I can't imagine what it must be like to have done something hundreds of times in my life and then suddenly realize that I didn't know how to do it any longer." Adam's voice was thoughtful.

"Isn't there anything we can do?" Sara wondered.

Neither Adam nor Mrs. Morgan had an answer, and all sat in thoughtful silence until Mr. Morgan joined them once more.

"What did Justin say?" Mrs. Morgan looked up to ask.

"He'll be up sometime tomorrow. An ambulance is coming to transport one of the patients to Jackson in the morning and he thought after that he'd be able to get away." He yawned. "I think I'm about ready to turn in."

"Dad."

Mr. Morgan turned from the fire which he was carefully banking for the night and looked at his son questioningly. "Yes?"

"Can I use the truck tomorrow?"

"All day?"

"Maybe. You aren't going to want it?"

Mr. Morgan shook his head. He could tell his younger son had an idea in his mind, but until he was ready to share it, his lips would remained closed.

* * *

It was late morning, and the winter sun was peeking through a partially overcast sky at the snowy world. A

bitterly cold wind was blowing in fitful gusts, as though complaining that the sun had come out, when Justin brought his truck to a stop before the Morgan home and climbed out. Attuned as he was to details, he noticed at once that his dad's truck was gone and wondered if Adam had taken it, since he had just gotten off the phone with his dad before heading up. Striding up the cleared walk, Justin glanced around. "Captain must be inside or Adam took him with him," he mused, not seeing the family dog anywhere. When he opened the door, the mouthwatering smell of Christmas cookies caused him to sniff with delight.

"I'm hungry already," he called, hanging up his coat and taking off his overshoes. It was a familiar call, one which he used to say every time he entered the house and something smelled good.

A laugh sounded from the kitchen and his mother's voice invited, "Come and taste one."

Justin wasted no time in accepting the invitation and, after his third cookie, asked, "Where is Amy?"

After shutting the oven door on another sheet of cookies, Sara swung Jenny up onto her hip as she answered, "She was reading in the living room the last I checked. She said she'd help ice and decorate the gingerbread men later."

"I help too," Danny grinned up at Justin before popping a piece of cookie dough into his mouth.

Justin laughed. "Well, surely you don't need me to taste test for you with such a willing and irrepressible taster right here."

"Oh, Danny!" Sara and Mrs. Morgan groaned together as Justin slipped from the room.

Finding Amy was easy. She was sitting on the couch

before the fire with a book in her hand, but she wasn't reading.

"Good morning, Amy," Justin greeted his patient, sitting down in a nearby chair and eyeing her keenly.

Slowly Amy looked up, her face sober, her eyes somewhat red. She didn't reply, but dropped her eyes back to the floor.

"How do you like it up here?" Justin asked casually.

"It's not working. I can't remember anything!" And Amy pressed her trembling lips together.

Leaning forward, Justin shook his head. "Amy," he chided, "you haven't even been out of the hospital for a week. You can't expect instant results."

"But I can't remember."

"I know. But you can live each day as it comes and move forward in life."

"Why can't I remember?" She looked up with pleading eyes brimming with tears. "Why?"

Dr. Morgan felt a deep sympathy for the girl and hesitated in his answer. He could sense she was fighting the urge to panic, and he knew sympathy would only make things worse. Therefore, his voice was light as he replied, "You don't want the scientific name for your condition, I hope! In plain English, something happens to the person, most likely a blow to the head of some sort, causing a temporary block in the part of the brain affecting memory. Some times this block only lasts a short time, say a few days to a few weeks. The person can remember things before that time and then there is a blank. Other times the block, like yours, shuts off all former memory leaving a person with a 'clean slate,' so to speak."

"When will it come back?" whispered Amy tearfully.

"That is a question the experts are still puzzling their

82

brains over. No one is quite sure. Sometimes these things last only a few hours, sometimes days, and sometimes years."

Amy gave a gasp. "I can't live like this for years! You've got to do something to fix it!"

"Amy," Justin's voice was quiet but steady, "if there was a way to bring it back, believe me, I would do it. But that's another mystery about the human brain. Sometimes it's a tiny thing that triggers a memory and suddenly the person recalls everything. Other times it is a slow, gradual process with bits of memory coming now and then. But no matter what happens with you," he paused and looked directly at the girl, "if your memory returns soon or if it takes a few years or if it never returns, you aren't alone. The best thing you can do for yourself right now is to decide that you won't give up. Jesus Christ is ready to help you each day, if you will let Him."

For a few minutes Amy was silent.

Justin, watching her somewhat anxiously, saw her shoulders droop and the book fall unheeded from her hand. Just as he was about to speak, Amy stirred.

"Isn't there any medicine that might help me remember?"

"No."

"Isn't there anything I can do to make my memory come back faster?" There was a desperate pleading in the tones.

"Perhaps. I don't know if it will bring back your memory any quicker, but I do know it will affect you for good if you will do it."

Quickly Amy straightened. "Tell me, Doctor, what is it? I'll do anything!"

"First off, you are to keep yourself busy and fill your mind with good things so there isn't much time to sit around and wonder and worry and grow upset. Help around the house when you are a little stronger, read, play with Danny and Jenny. There are probably many things you know how to do, if you stop trying to remember how to do them."

Amy shook her head. "I didn't even know how to set a table last night."

"That's probably because you stopped to think and then let yourself panic instead of asking for a little help. My Mother and sister want to help you if you need it, Amy. And so do the rest of the family. But you have to be willing to receive help." He paused to let his words sink in before going on.

~ 11 ~

"The second thing you can do is to keep cheerful. Giving way to despair and anxiety is not going to help you at all. Another thing is to eat." He frowned sternly though his eyes smiled. "I heard that you failed to eat a good breakfast this morning or much of a supper last night. That will never do. If I had wanted you on a starvation diet, I certainly wouldn't have sent you up here!"

Amy blushed slightly. "I—I'll try to do better," she promised.

"Good. Have you tried any of those cookies yet?" When Amy shook her head, Justin sprang to his feet. "I'll be right back. Stay where you are."

From the couch, Amy watched him disappear into the dining room and heard a low murmur of voices and some laughter. She didn't have time to wonder what he was doing, for in another moment he was back with several warm cookies on a plate.

"There you are!" Justin grinned, handing her the plate. "A sample of each one. You enjoy those while I have a look at your leg." His voice suddenly changed to that of Dr. Morgan and he asked, "Has it been bothering you?"

Later, after a hearty lunch was enjoyed, Justin leaned back in his chair and remarked, "Well, I'd better be heading back to town. Thanks for lunch, Mother." He stood up, hesitated, and then said, "On second thought, if you're planning on making more cookies this afternoon, I could stick around here and taste test some more."

Mrs. Morgan laughed. "If you stick around, you'll eat all the cookies."

"Can I help it if you make the best cookies anywhere?"

At that Sara straightened in her chair and retorted, "I'll have you know that I made the cookies this morning."

"But they were from Mother's recipes," countered Justin with a grin.

"They were from a cookbook."

"Well, then I'd better have a few more just to make sure they really are good," he teased.

"Justin Morgan, you stay away from those cookies!" Sara called, jumping up to give chase as her older brother disappeared into the kitchen, leaving Mr. and Mrs. Morgan laughing behind them.

"I thought those two had grown up," Mr. Morgan chuckled. "but apparently it was only a show."

Amy had watched in silence. This was certainly a strange family.

After Jenny and Danny were put down for their afternoon naps, Danny going reluctantly and insisting in the midst of his yawns that he wasn't tired, Sara mixed up the icing and brought the cookies out to the dining room table. Amy looked at the piles of gingerbread men and gingerbread ladies in amazement.

"What will you do with all those cookies?" she asked.

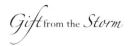

"We'll give many away, but you'd be surprised at how many Adam and Justin can devour. And when Heather and Timothy come over, well, let's just say we may have to make more before Christmas."

Amy blinked in wonder and reached for an icing bag.

"Do you mind if we put some Christmas music on?" Sara asked a moment later.

"No." Amy had filled her bag and placed a gingerbread man on the table before her. Still thinking about how many cookies there were, she gently squeezed the bag and began to ice. Finishing the first one, she reached for a gingerbread lady and quickly gave her a face, an apron and shoes.

"Oh, Amy!" Sara's gasp of surprise caused Amy to look up startled. "Those are so cute! I never can make mine look like anything but a mess."

Amy looked down at the two cookies. "I wasn't even thinking about them," she admitted. "I don't know where I learned to do anything like that, but I think I can do it again."

Sara watched as Amy bent over another cookie and soon had it transformed into a gingerbread man. "Do you like doing it?" she asked as Amy started on the second girl. When she nodded, Sara asked, hesitantly, "Would you mind working on them while I mix up a different kind of cookie? I'd help, but mine never look good and . . ." She lowered her voice to a whisper. "To tell you the truth, I hate icing cookies."

There was a smile on Amy's face as she replied, "I don't mind. I think this is fun."

With a sigh of relief, Sara hurried back into the kitchen, humming along with the Christmas song.

Left to her task, Amy became absorbed in each cookie. After doing a few exactly like the first ones she had done, she grew more adventuresome, adding a pocket on that one, a necklace on the next, cowboy boots and a collared shirt on another. She made some in nightclothes with their eyes shut, a few with funny expressions. On finding one with an arm broken off, Amy stuck it on with icing and finished it by making the arm look like it was in a sling. Thus inspired, she did a few others with bandages and chuckled softly at the result. When Sara saw them, she burst into a merry peal of laughter.

"Oh, Amy!" she giggled, "we'll have to save those and take them to the hospital staff." She laughed again. "Won't Justin and the others enjoy them!"

The afternoon passed quickly, and Amy was surprised when Mrs. Morgan brought the little ones downstairs after their naps. By then the gingerbread men were all finished, and Amy was washing dishes for Sara as she finished the last of the cookies.

"Well, it looks like you two have been busy," Mrs. Morgan smiled, looking into the kitchen.

Sara glanced up. "Go look at the cookies on the table." She nodded towards the dining room. "Amy did them all."

A sound of amazement came from the next room and then Mrs. Morgan exclaimed, "Amy, you are a wonder. How ever did you make them?"

Slightly embarrassed, Amy shrugged. "I don't know," she admitted. "But it was fun."

The family was almost ready to sit down for supper when the front door opened and Adam's voice was heard talking to Captain.

"Hurry up, Adam," Sara called, stepping from the kitchen into the hall. "Supper is ready."

"Be right there."

After supper the family gathered in the front room where Mr. Morgan, Adam and Sara helped Danny set up an elaborate train track for an old wooden train which used to be Justin's. Firewood was stacked up for a mountain and a footstool became a tunnel. Jenny was also interested in the train building, but her interests lay more in the destruction of the tracks. At last Mrs. Morgan carried her off to the kitchen where she was allowed to play with the pots and pans.

Amy, still pleased with her success in the cookie icing department, watched with interest the building of the tracks and at last suggested they use an old shoe box for a train shed. A box was quickly found and soon Amy was busy cutting out windows and a door which opened and shut. With this new addition Danny was pleased and spent at least ten minutes opening and shutting the door, driving his train in and out and looking through the windows.

"Honey," Mrs. Morgan said some time later, stepping into the room with Jenny in her arms, "do you know how late it is?"

Glancing up at the clock on the mantel, Mr. Morgan looked astonished. "I had no idea it was so late. Well—" He stood up and brushed his hands on his pant legs. "Let's have an evening song, some prayer and then call it a night."

Only one song was sung that night and when Amy heard it was her favorite of the evening hymns, she shyly joined in.

For some time after she had gone to her room, Amy

sat in the chair beside the window and gazed up at the bright moon and twinkling stars. Everything was so quiet and peaceful. She thought back over the day and wondered if perhaps, just perhaps, it might be possible to live a life in the here and now instead of trying to force the past into a mind that didn't want it. "Dr. Morgan said my memory might come back, but it won't help to worry and fret over it. Well," she sighed and rose slowly to her feet, "I'll try to do what he said. But it won't be easy, I'm afraid."

She crawled into bed, settling herself so that her face was in a pool of moonlight, drew a long, deep sigh, then relaxed and lay blinking in the soft glow until her eyes closed of themselves and she fell asleep.

There was a change in the atmosphere of the Morgan home the following morning when Amy limped into the dining room. The table showed signs of breakfast, but no one was around. Had she slept longer that she thought? Had something happened? As the last idea entered her mind, her muscles tensed and she looked wildly around the room. Gasping for breath, she gripped the back of a chair.

"Amy? What's wrong? Here, sit down." A chair was pulled out and Amy felt herself gently forced into it. It was then that she noticed Mr. Morgan's concerned face looking anxiously down at her. "What is wrong, Amy?" he asked gently, seeing her start to relax.

"I . . . I don't know. I didn't see anyone and . . . I thought something had happened, and I guess I panicked. I . . . I . . ." A shudder swept over her slight frame and she closed her eyes momentarily.

Mr. Morgan placed a gentle hand on her arm. "Everything is just fine. Today is Sunday and the others are getting ready for church. Mother is going to stay here with you today as Justin has forbidden you to go out just yet."

A slight look of surprise swept over Amy's face. "Sunday? I—" The sentence broke off suddenly. *She thought she heard the deep tones of the church bells ringing from the tower of the old stone . . .* It was gone. The sound, the picture, she shook her head with a sigh. "It's gone." Her words were listless.

"What's gone, Amy?"

"Church bells ringing, but the picture is gone."

Mr. Morgan frowned slightly. "You could picture the bells?"

"No, I could hear them." She put her hand to her head as though it ached. Why had the bells been ringing? Was it Sunday? Or were they ringing for— something else?

The sound of steps and voices were heard on the walkway above and Danny cried down, "Hi Grandpa!"

Mr. Morgan cheerily returned the greeting and then said softly, bending down so Amy could hear his voice, "I wouldn't fret over it, Amy; they'll ring again for you."

All was confusion for a few minutes before those headed for church were out the door, leaving Mrs. Morgan and Amy alone. A hearty breakfast was fixed for Amy and she ate it without much enthusiasm and almost in complete silence. The echo of the bells seemed to repeat themselves over and over and over in her mind.

It was a long morning for Amy with her usual distractions gone. Mrs. Morgan tried to interest her in talking, or reading, and Amy did her best to appear interested, but it wasn't until the others arrived back home that she was able, for a time, to forget the bells.

"Amy," Mrs. Morgan said, as Amy finished washing the last of the lunch dishes, "everyone takes a nap on

Sunday afternoon. You seem tired today, why don't you go ahead and lie down. Things will get lively later."

Nodding, Amy dried her hands and limped slowly from the kitchen, down the hall and into the cozy room she was growing to love. She felt worn out. But, as she closed her eyes, she heard the echoes.

Dong. Dong. Dong.

~ *12* ~

A few days passed and Amy seemed more content, more cheerful. Nothing had happened to upset or startle her and her smile was beginning to come readily when someone spoke to her. Though her leg was stronger, it still gave her twinges of pain now and then, at which times she was content to sit and read either to herself or to Danny who often demanded, "Read me!" When his demand wouldn't work with Sara or Adam, he would dimple into a smile for Amy and say, "Read me p'ease."

Amy seemed unable to refuse his request and would read until her voice was gone or until the young tyrant felt the need for action and would run off.

"Amy," Sara chided one morning after Amy had read the same two stories to Danny ten times, "you spoil that boy. You can tell him no."

With a shake of her head, Amy turned to watch the sturdy figure drive his train recklessly down the track and into the tunnel. "Maybe I should, but I can't seem to help it. I have a feeling of . . . well, I don't know how to explain it. It's almost like I've done the same thing hundreds of times before and it feels—right."

"You have read those books dozens of times at least.

Aren't you tired of the same ones? I am!" And Sara put the offending books back on the shelf. "I can't stand to read the same one over and over like you do."

Amy didn't reply. She knew she couldn't make Sara understand the feeling she got from reading to Danny.

The sudden barking of Captain out in the front caused both girls to turn and look out the large window. "That's Justin's truck! I wonder what he's doing up here in the middle of the week?" Sara quickly stuffed the scarf she was knitting into a bag and disappeared down the hall with it.

Still watching, Amy saw Adam come around the house and the two brothers stand talking. Neither had made a move towards the house before Sara came back.

"The difficulties of making Christmas presents," Sara remarked to Amy as she crossed the room to stand by the window, "is having to hide them every time that person shows up unexpectedly. Justin has always done that. Except," she amended, "when he was in medical school. Here they come."

A few minutes later the brothers entered the room and Danny raced over to them shouting and waving his train. Tripping over his sturdy shoes, Justin caught him before he fell. "You wild Indian," he laughed. "What do you have?"

"Train!" Proudly Danny showed his engine by shoving it in Justin's face. "Adam!" he shouted, squirming and wiggling in the arms that held him. "Play trains!"

Setting the little tyke back on the floor, Justin laughed. "You're in demand, brother."

"You'll have to wait a few minutes, Danny," Adam said in his calm, easy-going manner. "I have to fix the fire first."

At that, Danny forgot his train and ran over to watch. From the couch where she had been resting her leg, Amy looked on with a smile. Danny's endless energy often left her tired, but it was a good tired, she decided. Suddenly she straightened.

"Danny, no!"

Amy's words had been quick and firm. Danny jerked back his hand from the lovely glowing embers and turned to look at her. "Don't touch," was all she said, but Danny put his hands behind him and didn't touch a thing until Adam was ready to play trains with him.

"Well!" It was Sara's surprised exclamation which broke the silence. "I thought you couldn't say no to him. And I've never seen Danny obey so quickly when someone tells him no for the first or even the second time. How did you do it?"

There was no reply from Amy for a moment. She herself was surprised and a little confused by the whole thing. She had never told Danny no in her life, had she? "I . . . I don't know."

Justin must have read the look on her face, for when his sister started to say something else about it, he silenced her with a quiet, "Not now, Sare." And it wasn't until late that evening, after the little ones and Amy had retired to their beds, that he brought it up again.

"Adam, did you notice how quickly Danny obeyed Amy when she told him no?"

"Yeah."

"I didn't think Amy could tell Danny no." Mrs. Morgan looked questioningly at her sons. "What happened?"

Sara told the story quickly and added, "It reminded

me of when Timothy tells Brandon not to touch something."

A log snapped and hissed in the fireplace. "Do you think it means anything, Justin?" Mr. Morgan turned from watching the flames to look at his elder son.

"I'm not sure," Justin began slowly. "It seems as though Danny knows he has to obey Amy, but that leaves the question of why."

"When they were out in the mountains?"

"That doesn't seem to fit, Sara," Adam said slowly. "They might have been out there for days or a week, but the instant obedience seems too engrained for so short a time."

"That leaves before they came to the mountains or at least before they got lost." Sara tucked her feet up under her on the couch and folded her arms. "She isn't their mother?"

Justin shook his head. "No. If she was, Danny would have called her so, and Amy herself denied it. But she could be an older sister? A friend? A close relative?" With each suggestion, Justin looked around, hoping for a nod or another suggestion.

"I think I'd rule out friend."

"Why, Dad?"

"How often do children obey a friend of the family as quickly as you said Danny obeyed Amy?"

"Point taken. Sister? Relative?"

"Probably a good guess. I did a little checking on Saturday," Adam remarked. He looked across the room to his father. "I know you made inquiries in all the nearby towns, Dad, after they came, and in some of the nearby cities. But I thought it would be a good idea to actually talk to some of the folks there. I also wanted to check in some of the more out of the way places."

"Did you check the resort near Jackson?" Justin leaned forward and rested his elbows on his knees.

"Yep. No luck there. However, I did learn from a retired forest ranger something which might be of help." Adam paused and poked at the fire. "About a week or so before Amy arrived here, there was an avalanche farther up in the back range. It was bad." He stirred the fire before continuing. "Three hikers were lost. They only uncovered their bodies right before Thanksgiving."

A gasp came from Sara. "Do . . . do they know who they . . . were?"

"Two of them were from out of state, the other was local. The ranger couldn't give me any names, but suggested I check with the police in Jackson. I just haven't had the chance to get there yet."

"You can use my truck if you need to, Adam," Justin offered. "In fact, maybe I'll just go with you."

"And leave the hospital?" Mrs. Morgan shook her head. "Don't you have patients?"

Justin gave a groan and leaned back. "Yeah, but I'm finding I don't have much patience."

After Sara's first question, she had fallen into a thoughtful silence and gave no answering sally to her brother's last comment. Into the midst of the men's talk about which truck Adam should use the following day, she said, "So, if they were related, and Amy managed to escape from it with the children, are they the only family? Or are there any surviving relatives who think they were all killed in the slide?"

"I suppose we won't find the answer to that until we find out who the two people were," Mr. Morgan replied quietly. "Why don't we have a word of prayer for Adam's venture and then get to bed. It is growing quite late."

Justin paced the limited floor space of his office, glancing down now and then at the time on his watch. Had Adam arrived in Jackson yet? Would he find the right people to talk to? Were those victims related to Amy? If they were, what a tragedy for all three! A new thought struck him. What if the two who had died had been the parents of Danny and Jenny? Could Amy be a cousin or maybe a step-sister? Why didn't Adam call?

"Morgan, what's going on?"

Justin halted his steps and looked towards the door. "Oh, good morning, Hollend. It's nothing really. I'm just trying to make the time pass more quickly."

"For some particular reason?" Dr. Hollend stepped into the office and stood regarding his friend and fellow physician with a quizzical look.

"Adam's gone to Jackson." He glanced at his watch again.

"Christmas shopping?" Hollend's casual tone had the effect he had planned.

With a start Dr. Morgan looked back up and wet his lips. "No! He might have discovered something about Amy and the children."

"Really?" Dr. Hollend was all attention and Justin quickly told of Adam's reason for making the long trip to the city. "That could turn into something, but, Morgan, what if it doesn't? What if those two people had no connection with your trio, what then?"

With a sigh, Justin gripped the back of his chair. "Then we're back where we started."

"And if they are, or were, related, what are you going to do?"

"Find out if there are any kin."

"Does Dr. Stern think her memory will come back?"

"He doesn't know. No one does with these things. But if it was an avalanche that sent her and the children to us, maybe the talk of it would trigger her memory."

For a moment both doctors were silent, thinking of the stranger with no remembrance of the past. Then Dr. Hollend spoke. His voice was low. "What a thing to remember suddenly. Morgan, is she a Christian?"

Justin shrugged, his face grave. "I don't know. She doesn't know. But I have a feeling that whatever is keeping her from remembering is going to take faith and prayer to get through when she does remember."

"Then you don't think it was just a simple thing like a bump on the head?"

"No—from some of the things she said when she was sick and later mentioned, she had to get the children out of something dark or bad, but she couldn't remember what."

"Well, my wife and I will keep praying for her. And all of you. But it's time I made my rounds. Don't wear the floorboards out, Morgan." And with those parting words and a quick smile, Dr. Hollend disappeared down the hall.

"I should get busy," Justin muttered to himself, sitting down and pulling a file closer and flipping it open. "I do have work to do. But I wish I were in Jackson!"

It was late afternoon. There had been no word from Adam, and Justin felt as though he couldn't wait any longer. "This is worse than Christmas mornings," he complained to Dr. Hollend and Dr. Wright. "I'd wake up at three o'clock, often earlier, and I wasn't allowed to wake anyone up until five-thirty! Those were the longest hours I ever spent until today."

"There's no need of you staying around now," Dr. Wright reminded him. "You're off duty, you know."

"You're right. Maybe a walk will calm me, not to mention make the time go by faster." He picked up his coat and slipped his arms in. "Call me if you need me."

"Where will you be?"

For a moment Dr. Morgan looked blank. "Um, either at my rooms or at Dad's office. I'm not planning on going up to the cabin tonight unless I need to."

By the time Justin had reached his dad's office, which was only half a dozen blocks away, he was feeling rather numb. He'd forgotten just how cold winter was in the mountains, and the bitter wind took no mercy on him. Pushing open the door and stepping inside, he let out an involuntary sigh of relief.

Mr. Morgan looked up. "Any news from Adam?"

"I was going to ask you the same question. I haven't heard a thing!" Pulling off his coat, Justin hung it up and then dropped into a chair. "Why haven't we heard anything, Dad?"

"Did you expect him to call you from a pay phone?" Mr. Morgan questioned quizzically.

"Not really, it's just—"

The opening of the outer door interrupted him mid-sentence.

"The wind's picking up. We'll have to make sure we head home before it gets much later, Dad." Adam's calm voice brought Justin to his feet in a flash.

"What did you find out?" he demanded, whirling around to face his brother.

~ 13 ~

Adam didn't prolong the suspense, but said exactly what he had to say as though he had rehearsed it all the way from Jackson. "Philip and Amanda Smith. Age: mid-forties. Authorities are still trying to contact only kin which is an aunt or maybe cousin in Vermont. Police have no idea if they had any children."

"Smith? That's what Amy said her name was!"

"Justin, do you know how many people have the last name of 'Smith'? And remember Amy also told you first that her name was Jones." Mr. Morgan hated to shatter his son's hopes, but they had to be realistic. "Just because their last name was Smith doesn't mean they are related to Amy or the children."

Justin turned to his brother who had remained standing with his coat still on. "Did you find out anything else?"

"No. But let's just say, for argument's sake," Adam shrugged off his coat and sat down, "that Amy was related to them. How?"

Mr. Morgan relaxed and rested one arm on the back of his chair. "If the couple were in their mid-forties, Amy could be a daughter. Wouldn't you say she is about nineteen or twenty, Justin?"

Justin nodded. "Give or take a year or two."

"If she is a daughter, then the children could be— adopted family, or maybe step-children?"

"What about foster kids, Dad?" Adam asked. "Neither Jenny nor Danny looks much like Amy."

"Then the state they were from would have a record and would probably be looking for them, I would think."

"Perhaps Amy is a daughter-in-law of the couple." Justin frowned in thought. "Though she wasn't wearing a wedding ring, and I saw no marks of one."

The three men fell silent as the bewildering suppositions swirled around like a snowstorm. The problem was, they had no way of knowing if any ideas they had were even close to being right.

"This is more complex than a mystery novel," Justin sighed. "At least with them you can read the end if you get too confused."

"Or you can skip your chores to keep reading," Mr. Morgan retorted dryly. "As you used to do. Adam, we'd best be heading home. I don't think hashing over everything again will help. We'll just have to wait until the relative is contacted."

Adam nodded and rose to put on his coat. "I left information with the police and they promised to get in touch with us as soon as they hear anything. Good night, Justin. Don't stay up stewing over it all for too long."

"I won't. And thanks, Adam." Justin had put on his own coat and followed his brother out into the bitter wind while their father locked up the office.

Alone in his rooms, Justin Morgan sat before his table where the remains of his supper still lay. Though he had told Adam he wouldn't stew over everything, he couldn't keep his mind from replaying and analyzing every angle of Amy's life that he knew and seeing if it would fit with the couple who had died in the avalanche. Ever since Adam had returned from Jackson with the news, Justin could think of little else. After his father and brother had driven back home, he had walked nearly to his boarding place before he remembered his truck. Feeling rather foolish and cold, he had trudged back to his father's office and picked up his truck. Then, somehow, he had managed to fix himself a simple supper which he had eaten while absorbed in his thoughts.

When the clock struck eleven, he roused himself and stood up with a yawn. "Okay, there isn't anything I can do until we hear back. I can't sit here thinking about it all night." With no one to talk to in his solitary rooms, Justin often talked to himself. "Come on, Justin, clean up these dishes and get to bed. You have to work tomorrow. Forget everything Adam told you." This was easier said than done, and it required some time on his knees before he was able to go quietly to sleep.

The days which followed were ones of much wondering, conjecturing and restless waiting for the Morgan family. All were anxious to learn if Amy's only close relatives had perished in the rock slide. But, though the family questioned each other about the possible family connections, no one said a word of it all around Amy. Justin was not taking any chance of a set back before he knew the facts.

The days passed, turning into a week, and still no word from the police in Jackson. Christmas was coming closer and that fact helped push some of the wonderings aside, at least for Sara.

Sara Morgan loved Christmas. Every day she was busy, baking cookies or special breads, knitting or sewing presents, playing Christmas music on the radio or suddenly dashing off some Christmas tune on the piano. Her delight in the coming event infected Amy who looked forward to what she called, her "first Christmas."

* * *

One day Heather and Timothy came up to the cabin with their three children. Amy felt shy on meeting them but was soon at her ease as no one asked any questions besides the usual "how are you?" The children got along well, sharing and playing with only a few tears, and Sara and Heather pulled Amy into the kitchen to help with supper, leaving Mrs. Morgan to spend time with her grandchildren and Danny and Jenny. Right before supper was ready, Justin appeared. It was a large, noisy gathering around the Morgan table that night, and Amy found herself wishing she could stay there forever.

It wasn't until Amy and Sara were washing the dishes together that Amy discovered the reason for the visitors.

"Tomorrow we are getting our Christmas tree," Sara bubbled, almost dancing across the kitchen in her excitement. "Every year Heather and Timothy come over and spend the night and then in the morning Dad, Justin, Adam, Timothy, Heather and I set off on snowshoes to find the perfect tree. Often we're gone until after lunch. If your leg was only well, you could join us." She reached for another dish to dry.

Amy smiled. It was nice to be wanted, but she felt

more at home with the things she was familiar with than tramping through a snow-covered forest. "What happens after you find it?" If she wasn't going, Amy wanted to hear all the details.

"The boys and Dad will cut it down, and we'll bring it triumphantly home. We'll have to set the tree in the garage to thaw until after supper. Then the fun begins!"

"Hand me your towel, Sare," Heather laughed, coming into the kitchen just then. "All you are doing is talking."

With mock indignation, Sara clung to her towel and replied, "I was drying dishes while I talked. You just haven't been here to see me."

Looking at the growing stack of dishes waiting to be dried and put away, Heather grabbed her own towel and retorted, "Well, you aren't fast enough to suit me. Now you may continue with whatever you were saying."

"I forgot where I was." Sara picked up a plate.

"What happens after supper?" Amy prompted, eager to learn what was in store for the coming day.

"Oh, yes. After supper the boys bring the tree into the living room and set it up. Then we decorate it! Beautiful lights, and balls, and twinkling stars, and strings of popped corn . . . And the smell of the tree just fills the room and— Oh!" She broke off to sigh with delight. "Heather, we'll have to make sure we take enough food for snacks as well as lunch tomorrow. There's no telling how long it will take us to find the tree."

"I don't think I'll go tomorrow, Sara."

Sara turned quickly and almost dropped the glass she had been drying. "Not going? Why? Aren't you feeling well? You're not—"

"No," Heather put in quickly. "No baby. But I don't think we ought to leave all the kids for just Mother and Amy to look after."

"But Heather," Sara was ready to argue, and flipping her towel over her shoulder, she put her hands on her hips, ignoring the rest of the dishes. "You said last year that you'd go again this year because you wouldn't have a little baby who would need you. You can't back out now!"

Amy finished rinsing the last dish and picked up another towel. "Heather," she ventured, "you should go."

Both Heather and Sara turned in surprise and the former asked, "You think so?"

Wiping a shining drop off an otherwise dry plate, Amy nodded. "Yes, we can take care of the children. And Sara would like you along."

"Oh, Heather, say you'll come!" pleaded Sara. "Please!"

Before Heather could respond, a new voice asked, "What's the commotion about in here?"

"Oh, Justin, can't you get Heather to agree to go with us tomorrow? She's objecting on the plea that it would be too much for Mother and Amy to watch the kids."

Snatching the towel from Sara, Justin joined the dish dryers with a laugh. "I can't see any reason for you to stay, if that's your only excuse, Heather. Mother and Amy are quite capable of watching the youngsters. But if you are still unsure, why don't we ask Mother and Amy?"

"Amy is the one who suggested it," Heather admitted. "But Mother—"

"Mother!" Justin stuck his head into the hall and called loudly. "Do you mind staying at home tomorrow and watching the kids with Amy?"

"Of course not. I thought that was what we were

going to do anyway," was the satisfactory reply.

Heather put up her hands in surrender. "All right, all right, I'll go."

The tree hunting crew set off the following morning right after a hearty breakfast, leaving the young children shouting and waving out the windows and a kitchen full of dirty dishes. Heather had had second thoughts about going and leaving all the work for her mother and Amy to do, but they both insisted it would be just fine. It also helped that the others were very insistent that she accompany them.

It took more work than Amy had thought to keep track of five energetic youngsters, but she was willing to read stories and do just about anything they requested, and the morning passed by quickly. So busy was she at lunch time that she forgot to eat until Mrs. Morgan set a plate before her. The naps which came after lunch brought a quietness both Amy and Mrs. Morgan appreciated.

Sitting in the stillness, Mrs. Morgan looked at Amy and said, "If you want to take a nap as well, you go right ahead."

Amy shook her head, fingering the fringe of a blanket draped over the back of the chair. "I think I'd rather enjoy the quiet and not sleep it away."

"I know what you mean. Sometimes when my children were young, nothing rested me more than sitting alone for ten whole minutes. Amy, you look as though you want to ask me something. What is it, Dear?"

"I . . . I . . . What should I call you? I feel out of place here, yet at the same time this is feeling like home, but—"

Mrs. Morgan reached out a hand and placed it gently on Amy's arm. "If you'd like, Dear, just call me Mother like the others do."

At that Amy's eyes filled with tears. "Oh, may I?" She clasped the hand resting on her arm and emotion kept her voice in check for a full minute. Then she whispered, smiling through the tears which trickled down her cheeks, "I don't know if I have a mother living, I don't remember, but being here makes me wish I really belonged. I've wanted to call you 'Mother' since I first heard Sara call you that, but I didn't belong."

Mrs. Morgan, her own eyes dim with tears, moved closer on the couch and put an arm around Amy's shoulders. "You poor child, you do belong here now. God brought you to us for some reason that none of us know, and if you'll let us, we'd like to be your family."

For a time Amy basked in the feeling of belonging which was so foreign to her. Then a thought came to her. She sat up and clasped her hands tightly. Lifting frightened, pleading eyes to Mrs. Morgan she gasped, "What if—I remember?"

"We'll still be here for you. Amy, you are not alone. You'll have a home here as long as you need one. I promise. And this is not just a home, we are your family now, if you'll let us try and fill that role."

Amy nodded, too overcome to speak.

"Amy," Mrs. Morgan continued, drawing the trembling girl closer to her, "there is Someone who will never leave you, nor forsake you. Someone who gave His own life for you and for me. Do you know Who I am talking about?"

"Jesus." Amy whispered the name softly. "I have been reading the Bible in my room and the story of Jesus sounds familiar, yet new. I don't remember any of it, but when I read it, it all sounds right, like I already know the story. What does that feeling mean?"

Mrs. Morgan was silent. What did it mean? "Perhaps you read these stories before you came to us. Maybe that is why they seem familiar."

~14~

Restlessly Amy fiddled with a button on her sweater. She would have to think these things out herself when she was alone in her room. "Thanks, . . . Mother." The smile that came with the low toned word was half shy. "I think I'll—"

The sound of voices coming from the garage interrupted, and in another minute Sara and Heather, with faces glowing from the cold, and eyes sparkling like stars, entered the living room.

"We found a beauty!" Sara exclaimed.

"Shh," her mother warned, "the children are all sleeping."

Sara clapped her hand over her mouth. "Sorry!"

"The guys are putting the tree in the garage and then they'll be in." Heather rubbed her hands before the bright blaze. "Can we fix some hot chocolate for everyone, Mother?"

"And cookies," Sara added, "we must have Christmas cookies."

"Of course." Mrs. Morgan stood up. "One of you help me get it. Amy, you stay put."

Heather quickly followed her mother into the kitchen

just as the rest of the Christmas tree expedition came in.

"Shh," Sara told them. "The children are sleeping. Heather and Mother are bringing hot chocolate and cookies."

Amy watched in silence as Mr. Morgan, Justin, Adam and Timothy settled themselves around the fire. When the hot drinks and cookies came a few moments later, the room became filled with talk, mostly from Sara, about finding the perfect tree and where they went. Listening with only half a mind, Amy slowly sipped her hot chocolate and wondered what it would have been like to grow up in such a friendly, loving family.

The noise level in the Morgan cabin was quite high before supper when the tree was brought in. It hadn't thawed all the way so the decorating had to wait until after supper. With five lively youngsters, this waiting was filled with games of hide-and-seek with the men and Aunt Sara, in which none of the children could stay in their hiding places until they were found. Supper time brought a more subdued volume, but only until the young stomachs were filled.

At last the time had come. The lights were put on by the men and then the ornament boxes were opened. Amy enjoyed hanging the ornaments as much as the children. After Sara had started a few Christmas songs on the piano only to leave off in the middle of them to fly back to the tree, Justin took over the music, not only playing, but leading the others in one carol after another. Amy found herself singing right along, though when she stopped to think about it, she didn't know a single word.

At last the tree was decorated. The other lights in the room were flipped off and the family stood around

breathing in the enticing aroma of the pine sap, and admiring the lights twinkling and flashing off the glass balls and silver tinsel.

"Oh, Christmas tree, oh, Christmas tree," Justin's voice started the old song and the others joined in.

"It's the most perfect Christmas tree we've ever had," Sara sighed with delight when the song was over.

"You say that every year, Sara," Justin teased.

"Well, it's true—this year at least," she defended herself. "Don't you think so, Heather?"

"I think it's time certain little people were in bed."

Good nights were said and the family separated, each heading to his or her own room. Amy, lying under her warm blankets some time later heard the low murmur of Heather and Timothy's voices in the room next to hers. Closing her eyes, Amy felt a sense of security as the low voices came through the wall. She thought she could almost picture a different room; it was on the edge of her mind, but when she tried to focus on it, it slipped away leaving her with only the restlessness of a forgotten something. "If I can't remember what I want to remember," she told herself, opening her eyes and lifting a hand to the curtain, "I'll think of something else."

The sky was overcast and not a star was to be seen, nor the moon. Tiredly she let the curtain drop and settled back in her bed. The day had been busy, and her mind was whirling. "Can I really call her Mother?" she thought, recalling her talk with Mrs. Morgan. "Somehow it doesn't come easily. I want to say it, but I can't seem to make it come. Does that mean I don't have a mother? What about Dad?" She tried whispering it. She met with no more success than she had with Mother. "Maybe try Uncle, or

Aunt? I know Grandma and Grandpa are easy when I'm talking to Danny, Jenny or the other children."

Like many tired minds, Amy's soon turned to a different subject. "The Bible must be a book I've read before because it sounds so familiar. Jesus healed many people, but I haven't read any story of anyone like me. What did they do with people back then who couldn't remember?

"Perhaps someday I'll have to leave here. What if I saw someone I used to know?"

"I will never leave thee nor forsake thee."

Amy half sat up in bed. Where had that thought come from? Then she remembered. It was a verse Adam had read that morning at the table. Why had it come to her just then? She pondered the verse. If God was always with her, He must know her past. Why had He allowed it to be blocked in the first place? But what if she didn't love God? What if she wasn't a Christian. For some reason she was sure you had to be a Christian to have God always with you.

"Oh," she half wailed into her pillow at last, "I don't know!"

The talking in the next room had ceased and Amy knew it must be late. "I have to get to sleep," she told herself decidedly. "I'll just repeat the evening hymns. I missed singing them tonight."

"It's still a lovely tree," Heather told her sister. It was a gloomy morning, but everyone was up. The two Morgan sisters were standing in the living room together. "I was wishing our house in town had such a high ceiling, but since I know we'll be up here again, I'll just admire this tall tree."

"I can't believe Dad actually agreed to such a huge

one," Sara chuckled gleefully.

"And I can't believe we carried it home!" Justin's voice behind them made his sisters turn. "My back still aches just thinking about it." He rubbed his back, though his eyes twinkled. "But it does look pretty."

A demanding little voice sounded near Justin's knees. "Read me!"

"Danny, where are your manners?" Justin asked, picking up the youngster who was clutching his favorite book. "How do you ask nicely?"

"Want down," the little boy suddenly exclaimed, squirming and wriggling. As soon as he was set on the floor, he ran over to Amy, who had entered, a kitchen apron over her dress and begged, "Read me p'ease!"

"Oh, Danny, which story is it, because breakfast is almost ready."

Danny held out his book and smiled.

Amy didn't notice the others in the room, but sat down in a nearby chair and Danny climbed into her lap. Almost at once Erin Louise, Brandon and little Lucas hurried over and scrambled into the chair or leaned against the arm of it to hear the story. "All we're missing now is Jenny," Amy laughed.

"Grandpa has her," Erin Louise stated. "They are going up and down the stairs, so she won't miss it."

"She's going to spoil that boy," Justin remarked in low tones and with a shake of his head. "Does she ever deny him a story when he asks? And how come he says please to her and to no one else?"

Sara repeated what Amy had told her about it "feeling right" to read to Danny. Ending with, "We know she can tell him no about some things."

"Justin," Heather looked earnestly at her brother, "I would say those children are related to Amy. The more I watch them together, the more I see a resemblance, and there seems to be a, oh, how do I say it? A 'naturalness' that Amy has with them and not with any one else. Have you noticed it, Sara?"

Sara nodded. "I've noticed something, but I couldn't have described it like you. I wish we'd hear something from Jackson."

There was no time for a reply for Mrs. Morgan came around the corner from the dining room. "There you are," she said, smiling at the children clustered around Amy's chair. "Breakfast is ready. Erin Louise, why don't you run and get Grandpa."

"Where's Timothy, Mother?" queried Heather as the trio by the Christmas tree crossed the room.

"He's been helping in the kitchen with Amy and me, that is, until Amy disappeared."

Standing up, Amy brushed back a loose strand of light hair. "Sorry, I got distracted."

Mrs. Morgan laughed. "That's all right, Dear. I told Timothy you were probably captured by some literary little people. But come or breakfast will get cold. Where's Adam?"

Justin volunteered to find him and strode away, whistling a Christmas tune.

Amy stood with Sara and the children at the window and watched as Heather and Timothy and their children drove away down the mountain. "It feels like everyone is leaving," Sara grumbled good-naturedly. "Justin's heading back to the hospital, and even Dad and Adam have to go into town for some reason. I'd ask why, but you never ask

questions like that when it's this close to Christmas."

"Why?" Danny asked.

"Because they might be buying your Christmas present, that's why." And Sara stooped to tickle the little fellow.

"What should we do with the rest of the day, Amy?" Sara asked, as the two girls turned away from the window.

"Read books," was Danny's positive solution.

"I didn't ask you," Sara laughed. "Maybe we should make more cookies or work on Christmas gifts."

"Me too!"

"Mine, mine, mine!" Jenny shouted her new word after Danny and then giggled until she fell down.

What actually happened was a noisy game of romp with Sara and the little ones as Amy looked on and half wished she felt like joining them.

"Okay, Adam, out with it!" Justin commanded. "I drove all the way back to town knowing you had something on your mind and now you've been here five whole minutes and haven't said a word about it!" Mr. Morgan and Adam had driven into town and were now in Justin's small set of rooms he called home. "Why didn't you just talk back at the cabin?"

"Calm down, Justin," Mr. Morgan chuckled. "Perhaps if you'd give your brother a chance to speak, he'd tell us what it was about."

Adam looked up then. "I heard from Jackson."

"When?"

"This morning. That's why I was in the office. The couple in the avalanche didn't have any other relative that the aunt knew of. She's not coming out. Since the couple has already been buried, she didn't think she needed to."

Sinking into a chair, Justin let out a long sigh. It was as though he had been holding his breath since the news had first reached him about a possible connection to Amy's past. "Well, I guess that leaves us at square one again." Resting one elbow on the table, he leaned his head on his hand. "Any other ideas?"

"Adam, was this an aunt on the man's side or the woman's?" Mr. Morgan, leaning against a doorframe, folded his arms.

"The man's. She told the police she didn't know anything about the wife's side. They'd been married about five years but she didn't think they had any children. At least she never got any news about any. Do you think it would do any good to talk with her ourselves?"

"I doubt it. And the police did say they couldn't find any other relatives, right?"

Adam nodded. "I'd say there wasn't any connection then, just circumstantial timing."

From his chair, Justin had been listening to the talk but staring out the window toward the mountain. "Adam, did you check the towns in every direction?"

"As many as I could get to, north, west and south. I didn't have time to drive over the pass and check there. You want me to try it?"

Justin looked questioning up at his dad. Should Adam try driving over the pass and asking around the towns and hamlets on the other side of the mountains?

"It'd be mighty hard getting to some of those places in winter, boys. Adam, you could probably check the larger town, but most of what's over there is small pockets of a few houses or isolated cabins. And you never know when a blizzard would hit. I'd hate to have you become stuck out in

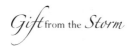

one far from shelter. Maybe you'd better wait until spring. Who knows, Amy might remember something by then and save you the trouble."

Silence fell over the three men. The search for Amy's past would have to wait until spring, unless she remembered something. Or if the inquiries Mr. Morgan had sent out only days after Amy and the children had been found, brought results. But as each day had passed, that hope was growing fainter.

"Justin," Adam asked, "have you ever asked Amy about some of the things she talked of when she was sick?"

"No. I've been almost afraid to mention them. A sudden shock could have been dangerous when she was still weak. I wonder if it would hurt now?" He lapsed into silence. And soon after, Mr. Morgan and Adam took their leave.

~ 15 ~

"Amy." A voice was calling through the door to Amy's room.

Groggily, Amy opened her eyes. Was it morning? It was still dark in her room and she was about to drift back off to sleep when the voice called her name again. "Hmm?"

"Amy, it's Sara, are you awake?"

"I think so."

The door opened and Sara put her head in. The soft glow of a light in the hall spilled into the room "Justin said you can come to church with us this morning, so you might want to get up now. Breakfast will be ready in about fifteen minutes." There was a smile in Sara's voice though Amy couldn't see it.

As the door shut, Amy sat up. Church? Justin had said she could go. Quickly she began to get ready, but paused suddenly in the hall. Did she want to go to church? There would be a lot of strangers and what would she say when they asked her where she came from? Maybe she should stay at home.

As she hesitated, Adam came into the hall from the garage. "Morning," he greeted her. "I expect the sun will be up above the horizon of clouds before we leave for church.

You'll get to see the mountain in all its winter glory when the sun shines. Hungry? I smell breakfast." Adam rarely said that much at one time, but his comfortable talk drew Amy along with him to the dining room and breakfast.

Her nervousness returned at the last minute when coats were being pulled on. Amy, halting in the doorway, said, "I . . . I think maybe I should stay here."

"Aren't you feeling all right, Dear?" Mrs. Morgan asked, placing a hand on Amy's forehead. "You don't feel feverish."

"Oh, you have to come," Sara pleaded. "Justin is playing the piano for the singing and you haven't heard him play much."

"Everyone in town knows about you, so there won't be any strange or awkward questions." Adam's quiet words were spoken just before he turned and carried Danny out to the car where Mr. Morgan was waiting.

Light dawned on Mrs. Morgan. "Were you worried about meeting strangers, Amy?"

Amy nodded.

"Oh, don't worry about that!" Sara impulsively put her arm through Amy's and half pulled her from the door. "Think of all the ones you will know. Mrs. Franklin should be there. Wasn't she one of your nurses? And probably some others. I don't know who is on call today. And probably one or more of the other doctors at the hospital." She kept up a constant chatter as everyone settled for the drive to church. "And don't forget Heather and Timothy. Why, Amy, there will be lots of people you know!"

Thus assured, Amy relaxed and began to take notice of the lovely landscape they were driving through. It was as Adam had predicted. The sun, rising above the bank of clouds which seemed to ring the world, turned the snow,

which only moments before had just been cold, white snow, into myriads of gleaming, sparkling, flashing diamonds. The pine trees stood as though wearing coats of white, glittering fur. Now and then a bird, landing on a small branch, would send a shower of crystal jewels cascading to the ground. Amy stared in awe at the landscape. She could hardly believe it was real. All this glorious, glittering, gleaming mass of snow was beyond words. She heard no sound, and had everyone around her been shouting, she wouldn't have noticed. Right then it was just her and the white world she was traveling through.

It wasn't until they reached the town and came to snow in dingy, gray piles, shoveled paths, footprints, snowmen in yards, and slushy streets that she drew a long breath and sat back in her seat.

Climbing from the car with the others, Amy looked ahead to the church building. There wasn't anything spectacular about it; it was just a typical country church with a high steeple and stone steps leading up to the doors. Up in the tower, the bell began to peal as the Morgan family made their way up the steps. At the first sound, Amy stopped and looked up.

She heard them again. *Dong, dong, dong. A white church spire. Dong, dong. Blue sky and piles of fluffy white clouds. Dong, dong, dong.*

"Amy," Justin called from the door.

"I'm coming, Matt." Amy's eyes dropped back and focused on the people before her. Seeing Justin waiting for her, she continued up and walked with him to the pew where she slid in next to Sara.

Moving up the aisle and seating himself at the piano, Justin puzzled over her remark. She had called him Matt.

Yet she hadn't seemed conscious of it. Her face had held an absent look as she gazed upwards. It was almost as though—Quickly he recalled himself and prepared to play for the opening song.

The minister's message that morning was tender as he dwelt on the lot of Mary and Joseph needing to make a trip, a difficult journey to another city, just to register for a tax. "I have often wondered what Joseph was thinking," the minister said. "Was he wondering why the tax had to come then? Did he fret about the trouble it would be to leave his business behind? Did he worry about his wife? There was no easy way of traveling back then. And Mary, did she sigh because her time was close and all her friends would be left behind? Or was she glad to go and get away from the talk which she knew was going on behind her back? Were Joseph and Mary familiar with the prophets who spoke of Bethlehem as being chosen to bear a light to lighten the Gentiles? Perhaps they did. Perhaps they were glad to go.

"But were they prepared to find nowhere to stay? I think not. There are many views about where they actually did stay, but whatever it was like, we know it wasn't a comfortable house. It was a place where they kept animals. They were not prepared for no room to be had for the birth of the Son of God. Jesus Christ was born in a poor, not overly clean, place because no one had room for Him. Mary and Joseph, they were surprised, I'm sure. But God wasn't.

. . .

"And still there are closed doors which say they have no room for Jesus Christ. There are lives which deny the Son of God a place. Some reject Him openly, turning their backs on Him. Some simply ignore the knocking at their hearts. But He is still there. He is waiting to come in, to enter a life, your life and give you His peace, His joy, His

love, if you will let Him."

There was more to the sermon, but Amy heard nothing else. How strange it would be to let someone live in your home and not know it. But she didn't know, had she opened the door of her heart? "I can't remember. I don't know. What if I haven't? But what if I have? Would I be insulting Jesus Christ if I asked Him to come in and He was already living there? That would be like asking a family member to come live in their own home. That wouldn't be good." She frowned slightly. "But . . ." Around and around her mind went, puzzling over the question. She would just have to ask someone. But who?

She looked up at the minister. No, she couldn't talk about it with him, even if he did look kind and friendly. Glancing down the pew, she inwardly shook her head. Sara wouldn't do. She was too light-hearted. Amy was still a little shy of Adam and Mr. Morgan. Should she ask Mrs. Morgan? No, she decided. She'd only worry her. She was a wonderful, motherly person, but—Justin?

The ride back to the cabin wasn't nearly as silent, for Sara chattered about who she had talked with and what was going on in town. "Amy, doesn't Justin play the piano well? I used to think he'd be a concert pianist, but then he went off to medical school. But he still plays. He said he used to play every evening in the dorm before he went and studied, and he played other places, but still. Adam, Ron asked me when you were coming over to help him finish some project. I told him I didn't know, but you were busy talking to Mr. and Mrs. Burton. Mother, I think I'll have to make more cookies since Justin is coming for lunch. Is he staying for supper too?"

"I don't know, Sara," Mrs. Morgan replied. "You'll have to ask him."

"If Justin is staying for a while," Amy thought, "perhaps I'll have a chance to talk with him."

That chance came after lunch. The children were put down for naps in spite of Danny's protests, and soon after, Mr. and Mrs. Morgan slipped away. Sara retired to the kitchen humming Christmas music and Adam said he was going for a walk with Captain. This was just what Amy wanted, but she didn't know how to start.

"Amy," Justin broke a silence which was growing long, "what were you thinking about before church, when you were listening to the bells ring?"

Tucking her feet up on the couch, Amy noticed that her once injured leg didn't bother her. "I kept hearing church bells from somewhere, when people talked about Sunday or church . . . and then, this morning, I could picture it. It was a white steeple and the sky was so blue and the clouds . . ." Her gaze grew far away and her voice trailed off.

Justin almost held his breath. Was she remembering?

Amy sighed. "And that's all I can picture. I wonder why I have that picture in my mind. You can't exactly find the right steeple because there are probably thousands of them in the country, and the sky doesn't help any either or the clouds."

With a slight chuckle, Justin replied, "No, I'm afraid things like that won't help. But tell me, do you know who Matt is?"

~ 16 ~

Amy looked at him blankly. "No, should I?"

Justin moved his chair closer to the couch. Keeping his eyes on Amy's face to catch the slightest change of expression, he said, "You called me Matt this morning before church."

"I did? When?"

"When I called you from the doorway. You were staring at the steeple."

Amy shook her head. "I don't remember anyone saying anything to me. At least I didn't hear it. Matt?" She frowned. "Have I talked about 'Matt' before?"

"When you were delirious you talked about Matt and Kathleen." He paused and waited, but when no look of recognition or remembrance came to Amy, he went on. "In fact, you talked a lot about many things that didn't make any sense. But don't worry," he added quickly as a troubled looked began to steal over the girl's face. "Anyone who suffers from as high a fever as you did is bound to say strange things. And sometimes they have nothing to do with anything."

Amy relaxed and stared at the floor. "I . . . I have a question I wanted to ask . . ."

"Okay, what is it?" Justin leaned back in his chair appearing completely calm, though he was disappointed that the names hadn't brought any reaction from Amy.

Instead of asking, Amy fidgeted with a pillow and began picking imaginary pieces of lint off her skirt.

Justin waited in silence.

The sound of Christmas songs being sung in the kitchen could be heard and the soft crackle of the fire. The fragrance of the Christmas tree over by the window brought with it a feeling of excitement about the coming holiday. At last Amy spoke, her voice so low and hesitant that Justin leaned forward in his chair again. "What if—I was already—a Christian before—this—happened—and I don't—remember? Would it be—insulting to—Jesus Christ if—I asked Him—to come into my life—and save me—again?"

The reply came quickly. "No, Amy. Jesus Christ knows all about you. He knows you can't remember things right now, and He wants to help you. Even if you already asked Him to forgive your sins and to come into your life, He won't mind if you do it again. And, Amy, if you have never done it, He is waiting for you to let Him in. He loves you, Amy, whether you remember Him or not."

Her dark eyes were focused on Justin's earnest face. "Are you sure He wouldn't mind being asked a second time to forgive someone? I thought about it in church, and I know people would get offended if they were asked to do something they had already done."

"Amy, God is not like us. His love is unending and His mercy is so great we can't comprehend it. If He told his disciples to forgive someone seventy times seven, don't you think He would do the same? All you have to do is ask."

Moving restlessly, Amy turned her head away and

stared at a picture hanging on the far wall. It was a family picture of the Morgans before Heather got married, and suddenly Amy burst into tears. She buried her face in her arms on the back of the couch and cried. "I just want to remember! I want to know who I am and where I belong!"

Justin rose and placed a hand on her shoulder. For several minutes he didn't speak. "Oh, Amy, how I wish I could bring your memory back to you. But I can't. All I can tell you is to go to Jesus Christ. He will never leave you nor forsake you. You can know one thing for sure, Amy, if you give yourself to Christ, you will be a child of the Most High. You will belong to Him and with Him forever, and nothing can separate you. Not life, not death, not even the lack of memory."

Amy's sobs had lessened as Justin talked. A muffled response of some sort came from the bent head.

"What was that?" Justin leaned forward. "Amy, I can't understand you with your face buried." He sat down on the couch beside her. "Come on," he coaxed. "Things aren't so bad when you come right out and face them. But hiding from them, afraid to look at them, is worse than not turning on the light when you are afraid there is a bear in the closet."

One arm moved and Amy's face became partially visible. She fumbled in her pocket and pulled out a handkerchief. Still keeping most of her face hidden, she sniffed, "But you don't know who I am."

Justin raised his eyebrows questioningly. "I'm not sure I follow you."

"The me before I came here. What if I was a terrible person? What if—what if I kidnapped Danny and Jenny?"

A chuckle came from Justin at that. "I don't think

there's any cause to think that, Amy. The way the three of you act together is not how a kidnapper and the kidnapped would act. Why Danny adores you and Jenny lights up whenever you enter a room. No, kidnapping is out of the question."

"But what if I killed someone? What if I'm a hit and run driver? Or am wanted by the F.B.I.?"

"Amy, quit being dramatic," Justin scolded. "The past is behind you. Jesus said, 'He that cometh to me I will in no wise cast out.' And in John 3 it says 'For God so loved the world, that whosoever believeth in Him should not perish, but have everlasting life.' Now, even if you were any of those things, and I'm as sure as Sara is making ginger cookies," he sniffed the air, "that you are no murderer, kidnapper, swindler, fugitive or any other thing you might imagine, don't you think that when Jesus says, 'whosoever' He means it?"

Amy sniffed and gave a faint nod.

"And if He means it, are you going to be the one who says, 'not so, Lord'?"

The bowed head was shaken this time.

Earnestly Justin pleaded his Savior's claims. "Why don't you just come to Him now? Forget the past. Don't try to know if you belonged to Jesus then, or get stuck wondering what you may have done wrong. It is the here and now that matters. Amy, you have to live *now*, you have to decide *now*! The past is behind you. When you are a child of God, He takes all your sin away, even the things you might have done in a past you can't remember. Won't you come to Him now?"

The silence was long. Sara came to the doorway but paused and then, without a word, slipped away again. A log in the fireplace broke sending sparks soaring up the chimney, and on the mantel, the clock struck the hour. Still there was no word from the girl on the couch. Only occasional sniffs sounded. Justin waited and prayed. He could only imagine what torture it must be for a mind to go through what Amy had been through. Everything she had been taught, if she had been taught anything about the Bible, hidden, because her mind refused to remember.

At last Amy lifted her tear stained face. Her dark eyes were full of longing, pain, and fear. "I want to belong," she whispered. "I want Christ to be with me no matter what. Help me." She put out her hand as though asking someone to lead her, and Justin took it.

Up above on the walkway, Mr. Morgan glanced down and paused. Justin and Amy were kneeling by the couch. Turning swiftly, Mr. Morgan retraced his steps to his room and in a few minutes, he and his wife were also on their knees praying for the lonely girl who had come to their home so many weeks ago and rejoicing that she had found help.

That evening, for the first time, Amy sang the evening hymns with the others and knew she meant every word. She spoke no word of what had taken place in the living room that afternoon, but her face wore a look of peace not seen earlier.

Before she crept into bed, she opened her curtain and gazed for a moment at the bright, twinkling stars, the glimmering snow and the pools of light spilling forth from the dining room windows. "A Baby was born and all is right with the world," she thought with a smile. "Well, maybe not the world," she amended, "but with me." Looking up into the starlit heavens she whispered, "I am Christ's and Christ is mine!"

* * *

The days which followed were busy ones. Amy marveled at all the things Sara managed to come up with to make the house more festive. At her request, Adam had brought home a sled full of pine branches, and with them Sara created a wreath to hang on the chimney. This was followed by one for the front door. Danny and Amy helped make paper chains and Mr. Morgan and Adam hung them from the rafters in the living room and they gave the room such an air of festivity that Sara burst into "Deck the Halls" while Amy kept Danny from climbing the ladder as Adam hung the last chain. Everyday the excitement built until Amy wondered if the whole house would burst before Christmas Day arrived.

In the late morning of Christmas Eve, Timothy and Heather arrived with their children. Erin Louise, Brandon and Lucas begged to make paper chains too.

"Of course you can make more paper chains!" Aunt Sara agreed, and soon the children, with the exception of Jenny, were established at the dining room table.

"Sara, where are we going to put more of those things?" Adam questioned in a low voice.

"I don't know yet," Sara laughed. "I'll think of somewhere. Or Amy will. Oh, it's a wonderful day! And Adam." Her younger brother turned around. "It's snowing!"

"You'd think she was nine instead of nineteen," he muttered to Heather as he passed her in the kitchen.

Heather only laughed while Amy suggested they hang

the new chains from the walkway on either side of the fireplace.

Justin arrived mid-afternoon. "It sure is snowing hard out there," he remarked, stepping into the living room. "I wasn't sure I was going to make it up here. But now that I'm here, I don't know if I'll be able to make it back down, at least not until they've plowed the main road."

Mr. Morgan looked up from the book he had been reading. "Is it really that bad?"

"Visibility is pretty limited." He held his hands to the warm blaze. "Where is everybody?"

With his finger in his book to mark the page, Mr. Morgan replied, "The children are napping, Adam and Timothy went off somewhere, and I think the girls are in the kitchen. You can go bother them if you want."

Taking the hint, Justin slipped off to the kitchen, leaving his father to return to his book. He found both his sisters and Amy in the kitchen.

Heather looked up when he entered. "Hi, Justin. How were things at the hospital?"

"Slow. Actually there's only one patient. Mr. Flannery from over near Mustang Meadow. Dr. Wright is staying there tonight. Since his family all lives back east, he said he'd rather spend Christmas at the hospital than at home alone. At least this way he'll have a few people to talk to.

"What are you all making?" He picked up a slice from the apple Amy was cutting.

"Pies for tomorrow. We're going to—Justin Morgan, stop eating the apples!" Sara scolded, shaking a spoon at her big brother.

"Oh, Sara," protested Amy mildly, "he's only had two little slices." Before Justin could thank her for taking his side, she added, "And if he eats too many now, tomorrow we'll take all the apple from his piece of pie and he can just eat the crust."

The laughter in the kitchen was merry over Amy's suggestion, and soon Justin, who missed this family time when he was in his lonely rooms in town, was busy washing dishes.

~ 17 ~

Amy enjoyed the evening with the talk and laughter over dinner, the singing around the piano later and finally gathering with the family while Mr. Morgan read the Christmas story. She looked around the room. It was all so cozy and special. Timothy and Heather sat together on the sofa, their hands clasped. In the two chairs opposite each other on either side of the fire were Mr. and Mrs. Morgan. Mrs. Morgan cuddled a sleepy Jenny in one arm, while her eldest grandchild sat on a stool beside her and leaned a tired head on her Grandma's knee. Lucas, sitting perfectly still, had the seat of honor in Grandpa's lap, while Danny and Brandon wiggled on the rug at his feet, trying to stay awake. From her corner of the couch, Amy looked at Justin's quiet face and then at Sara's expressive one. They were so alike and yet so different. It was easy to see the family resemblance. A slight movement on the other side caused Amy to turn her head. Adam was leaning forward in his chair and staring into the fire. He seemed to be lost in the story being read.

Amy relaxed and listened too.

Christmas morning came sooner than most of the

Morgan family wanted, for with Erin Louise and Brandon in the house, there was no chance to turn over and go back to sleep. Amy heard the first excited squeals from the next room and Timothy's low voice. Then the sound of pattering feet running down the hall. A knock sounded on her door and Erin Louise's voice called, "Merry Christmas, Aunt Amy! Hurry and get up so we can open our stockings!" Then aside to someone else, "Come on, Brandon, let's go wake up Aunt Sara. Lucas, we're going to get Grandma and Grandpa!"

"And Uncle Adam!" Brandon urged. "And Uncle Justin!"

The thud of little feet faded, and Amy sat up. Turning on her lamp she looked at the clock. It was five o'clock. Smiling, partially at the excitement the children had left behind and partially at her own eagerness about Christmas, Amy slipped from her bed and reached for her warm bathrobe. She remembered Heather's words from last night.

"Don't bother getting dressed right away, Amy. We always open our stockings in our bathrobes and slippers. We get dressed after that."

"This is certainly going to be an experience," Amy thought, opening her door and stepping out into the chilly hallway.

Everything was dim. Heather was just plugging in the Christmas tree lights and Timothy was lighting the fire when Amy entered the room. "Merry Christmas," she whispered.

They both returned her greeting and then voices and the thud of large and small feet was heard up above. Moments later the rest of the clan emerged into the living room, shuffling in slippers and trying to hide yawns. Jenny

clung to Sara, rubbing sleepy eyes, while Danny jumped up and down.

The excited squeals of the children when they caught sight of their overflowing stockings hanging from the mantel, made Justin put his hands over his ears. "I should have stayed in bed," he complained with a laugh to Heather and Amy. "Put us out of our misery, Dad!"

Mr. Morgan soon had the stockings handed out, but the noise level only increased as gifts were pulled out, unwrapped, and exclaimed over.

When at last the final stocking had been bereft of its treasures, the older members leaned back and looked at each other. They might be tired, but the day had only begun.

Sitting among her treasures, Erin Louise, her brown hair done up in rag curlers, asked, "Can't we open the presents under the tree now?"

"Not until after breakfast," her mother told her. "And you have to get dressed."

"Amy, just toss your paper on the floor with the rest of it," Sara instructed, seeing Amy begin to gather her crumpled and torn wrappings. "Those who aren't helping fix breakfast get to clear it all up. It gives them something to do." She laughed and tossed a paper ball at Justin. He returned it with better accuracy than his sister and Sara gave a little scream.

Setting the table not long afterwards, Amy listened to the chatter in the kitchen as Mrs. Morgan and her daughters prepared breakfast. The smell of pancakes, eggs, bacon and coffee invaded the dining room and made Amy realize how hungry she was, even if it wasn't yet seven o'clock. It was still dark outside and Amy had to lean close to the window in order to see outside. The snow must have stopped sometime during the night but a huge drift was piled against the side of the house, reaching above the window ledge. Never had she seen such a large drift and she wondered how deep it was.

"What are you looking at?" Justin asked.

"This snow drift. It comes up past the bottom of the window." Amy didn't turn but kept staring out at the heaps of snow.

Justin snapped the room light off and walked over. "That is deep." With the lights off it was easier to see into the dim early morning. "We've had some pretty deep drifts up here in the middle of winter. One year Adam and I kept a record of how deep the drifts were around the house. I wonder if Adam still has that paper." Musingly, he turned away and flipped the light back on.

Glancing down, Amy remembered the silverware still in her hand. "I'd better finish setting the table before it's time to eat."

Everyone was in good humor over breakfast and the large stacks of pancakes seemed to melt away until there were only half a dozen left.

"Does anyone want these?" Amy asked, glancing around the table while she rested her hand on the plate of leftover pancakes.

As groans and shaking heads answered her, she lifted the plate and set it before her.

"Amy," Sara gasped, "are you that hungry?"

"No. I'm not hungry a bit." She didn't notice the puzzled and astonished looks sent her way as she began tearing up a pancake. "Here, Danny, do you want to help me?"

"Yes!" was the eager answer, and Danny seized a

pancake and tore it into bits.

Glancing at his mother, Justin wondered what was going on. He was afraid to ask, fearing that Amy would forget what she was doing. This seemed so natural to her, as though she did it every year. But what was she doing?

If Justin and the other adults held back their questions, Erin Louise didn't. Getting up on her knees and leaning part way across the table, she asked, "What are you doing?"

"Tearing the pancakes. Do you want to help?"

"Yes, but why are you tearing them up?" persisted the little girl, slipping from her chair and coming around the table.

At this question, Amy's hands paused and a look of blank bewilderment swept over her face. She opened her mouth as though to say something, but closed it again as Brandon and Lucas crowded around to join in the fun.

"What are we going to do with them?" Erin Louise rephrased her question.

"Give 'em to the birdies" shouted Danny, holding both little hands up above his head and dropping the pieces of pancakes.

No one noticed Danny's action, for all adult eyes had been focused on Amy's face. At his words, relief and assurance replaced the look of confusion and she echoed, "Yes, we give them to the birds. Don't you think they ought to have a nice breakfast on Christmas morning?"

Erin Louise and Brandon nodded.

"I'm afraid, with all the snow we had yesterday and last night, anything you throw out for the birds will just disappear," Mrs. Morgan began. "Perhaps—"

"We can take the hint, Mother," Adam said, pushing

back his chair and standing up. "With four of us working, we can at least clear a little area."

"And while you men do that, and Amy keeps the little ones occupied collecting crumbs for the birds, Sara, Mother and I can take care of the dishes." Heather flashed a smile at her brother and picked up his plate, stacking it on her own.

So delighted were the children about feeding the birds that not a crumb seemed to escape their sharp eyes. The pieces from Jenny's highchair were collected and Brandon remarked that, "the birds would like some syrup on some pieces." Grandma produced a bowl for the children and Amy to use, since pieces of pancake kept falling from the overfilled plate. When the last piece was gathered, sticky hands and faces were washed before Amy allowed anyone to go watch the progress of the shovelers.

"You know," Heather remarked in a quiet voice, returning to the kitchen after a peek into the living room and setting down a dish she had just finished drying, "I don't think the children have even noticed the presents under the tree. They are too engrossed by the prospect of feeding the birds."

"Bless Amy for that inspiration!" Sara exclaimed. "Mother, do you think this is something Amy has done most of her life? It sure looked like she and Danny have done it before."

Mrs. Morgan put away the pan before answering. "I would guess that it was, Sara. If she had thought of it right then, I don't think she would have looked so confused when Erin Louise asked about it."

"This adds more evidence to my theory," Heather put in. "If Danny remembers doing this, then he and Amy must be related, and Jenny—"

"Is his sister," Sara interrupted. "Amy has called her 'Sissy' to Danny before when she is playing with them."

A shout from the living room interrupted the conversation, and the ladies, with dishes and towels still in their hands, hurried into the other room. Amy had given the bowl to Timothy, and the children, pressing against the window, were cheering as he tossed the pieces onto the shoveled area before the window and on the path before the porch.

"We'd better hurry and finish these dishes," Sara whispered, "or the boys will tease us that we don't work very fast."

It was a busy day. The opening of the presents under the tree took up most of the morning and then the litter of paper had to be cleared away.

"Remember the time," Sara began, crumpling a piece of wrapping paper into a ball, "that Justin and Adam thought they should burn the paper in the fireplace?"

"What happened?" Timothy asked, "I don't think I've heard this story."

"Oh, not that story, Sare," Justin protested. "Can't you think of something else? Like the time you just stuffed it all under the couch?"

Sara ignored his pleas and his suggestion, and, finding interested listeners in her brother-in-law and Amy, she launched forth. "It was a number of years ago. Justin and Adam had been told to clean up the paper after we had opened gifts and, since it was going to be burned later anyway, they thought they'd save themselves some trouble. I don't know which one started it, but they were both doing it when we saw them."

"Doing what?"

"Trying to throw paper balls into the fireplace. Some made it and quickly caught on fire, others missed completely, but then two were thrown at the same time and instead of staying in the fireplace when they caught on fire, they jumped or rolled out."

Amy gasped. "Still on fire?"

"Yep. And they rolled out of the fireplace and managed to catch two or three other balls on the floor on fire. Then Dad walked in the room. I think that's when they decided it wasn't such a good idea after all." She grinned at her brothers. "Wasn't it?"

Neither brother answered as both were industriously searching for stray bits of paper behind the chairs.

"How old were they?" Timothy chuckled. He hadn't grown up with any brothers, and the stories he heard now and then of his younger brothers-in-law amused him.

"Old enough to know better," Heather answered. "And so was Sara when—"

"Heather, don't you think we ought to start fixing lunch now?" Sara interrupted quickly, her face turning scarlet.

"No, we still have plenty of time. As I was saying, Sara was about seven and she had been told to—"

A loud chord was struck on the piano, interrupting the story. "I think we should all sing now," Sara suggested.

This was the last interruption her brothers would listen to, and Amy watched and laughed with the others as Adam shut the lid over the keys and Justin muttered threats to her if she even moved.

"You told a story on them," Heather reminded her with a grin, "so you should just sit and listen to one on yourself. As I was saying," she began for the third time,

"Sara had been told to clean up the paper. The boys were helping Dad and I was fixing lunch with Mother. Anyway, she didn't want to do it and so decided it would be easier to just stuff all the paper and things under the couch. She didn't think anyone would notice. And no one did. Until spring."

Amy glanced from Sara's bent head and flushed face to the wide eyed faces of the children. She wished she could tell a story about something that had happened to her.

"Every spring Mother gets the urge to clean the entire house. And believe me, Amy, it's no easy task! That year we had gotten as far as the living room, and Justin and Dad were moving the furniture so we could clean under everything. When they lifted the couch, imagine the surprise of finding Christmas wrapping paper all covered with dust and even some spider webs. Sara was the picture of shame that day."

"What happened?" Erin Louise whispered. "Did she get spanked?"

"No, but I think the punishment she did receive made more of an impression than a spanking. She had to pick up a piece of paper in each hand and carry it out to the trash pile and then come back and get two more. She was only allowed to take two pieces each trip, and by the time she was half way done, she was crying."

"That's a long walk for a seven-year-old girl to make over and over and over," Sara interjected. "After I had finally finished, Grandpa asked if I thought obeying the first time would have been better and easier."

The silence which followed was broken by Mr. Morgan. "What, moralizing on Christmas Day?" He leaned on the railing of the walkway and looked down on the group below.

"No, Grandpa, we not 'lizing' we just tellin' stories," Brandon chirped.

"And we're not going to put the paper under the couch or throw it in the fire," Erin Louise added with great decision.

Mrs. Morgan came into the living room tying on an apron. "If I can get some help, lunch will be ready in a few minutes."

Quickly Amy, Heather and Sara joined her to prepare the simple meal.

The rest of the day Amy found to be as enjoyable as the beginning.

~ 18 ~

After lunch and naps, in which everyone joined, there were games, and Amy read story after story until her voice was almost gone. Some of the others tried to coax the children into letting them read a story or two, but Danny wanted no one but Amy to read, and she, delighted to be so wanted, complied without a murmur.

A dinner of ham and potatoes, peas, green bean casserole, fresh rolls and apple butter, and four kinds of pie and Christmas cookies for dessert sent everyone to the living room feeling that they could skip all meals for the next week. Much to Amy's surprise, the ladies were banned from cleaning up and the men took over. "I thought the women always cleaned up the kitchen," she said in low tones to Sara.

"Not here they don't," Sara replied. "And I'm glad. I don't mind cleaning up regularly, but I enjoy these times when I don't have to wash another dish."

Justin had a new game to play after the dishes were done. Sitting down at the piano, he played a few chords and then said, "I'll play the first measure of a Christmas song and you all try and guess what it is."

This proved to be too easy for the musical family

members, so Justin changed things up a bit. "I'm going to leave off the melody and see if you can guess it."

That was a bit more of a challenge and then Sara suggested they sing.

"Sara, have pity on us," Adam begged. "I can't sing when I'm this full."

"Then what shall we do?"

Danny, who had climbed into Amy's lap, looked up at her and said, "Tell me story, p'ease."

"I don't know any stories, Danny."

"Just make one up," Erin Louise suggested.

"Why don't you make one up and tell it to us, Erin Louise." Justin had ceased his soft playing and looked over at his niece.

"I can't think of any. You tell a story."

In the end, Mr. Morgan told a story of when he was a boy and lived on a farm in the foothills. By the time the story was over, Adam declared that he thought he could sing and everyone gathered around the piano, And so, the evening ended with several beautiful carols and a prayer.

Alone in her room that night, Amy spread her gifts out on her bed and looked at them. They were not expensive gifts and most were homemade, but that didn't matter to her. She knew they had been made with love. Even Danny's childishly decorated picture frame was special, with his and Jenny's faces looking at her from inside. A sudden sob rose up in Amy's throat as she looked at the picture, and hugging it to her heart, she choked out, "Oh, little ones, I hope your mama isn't missing you this Christmas!"

* * *

Christmas had passed and so had the New Year. Amy was settling into life at the Morgan home with an ease that sometimes astonished her. Each day it became easier for her to call Mrs. Morgan "Mother" and Mr. Morgan "Dad," which delighted him.

"I always knew I needed another daughter," he told her with his fatherly smile. "Heather gave me another son when she got married, but it doesn't appear that Justin or Adam is going to marry any time soon."

One afternoon the wind picked up, and when Mr. Morgan drove in early from town, he called Adam. "I think we'd better bring in more firewood and make sure everything is tight around here. There's a storm blowing in, and if I'm not mistaken it's going to be a blizzard."

Adam nodded. "I figured one was moving this way from the way Captain was acting and by the look of the sky." Quickly he pulled on his boots and grabbed his heavy coat.

After they had stepped outside, Sara, who had been standing in the hallway, turned around, "Mother! Dad and Adam think we're in for a blizzard!"

"I heard them, Sara," Mrs. Morgan answered coming from the dining room. "There's no need to shout."

Sara turned at her mother's voice. "Sorry, Mother. I thought you were upstairs. Isn't there something we should do to get ready or should I help with the wood?" Pent up excitement tinged her voice and her eyes sparkled with adventure.

"Oh, go help with the wood if you'd like. I think Amy and I can get out a few more blankets and make sure the lamps have oil and the flashlights have batteries that work."

Sara needed no urging but was already pulling her boots from the closet before her mother finished talking. Sara loved adventure, and the prospect of a blizzard sent her feelings rushing as though on the wind itself.

It wasn't until the excited girl was outside that Amy, looking up from a book she was reading, asked, "Can I help do anything, Mother?"

"I help too," Danny insisted, rushing across the room from the tower he had been building for Jenny. "I help too, Grandma."

"All right. Let's get some extra blankets out of the linen closet. If the storm is bad, it could knock the power out and we might need some extra covers."

Amy was somewhat puzzled by the preparations, for she didn't know what a real blizzard was like. She thought they had already had several blizzards and they hadn't prepared like this before. "I would think it would get awfully cold here without heat. At least there is a fireplace. And I thought the oil lamps were only used on special occasions." She thought back to Christmas Eve when a few oil lamps had been lit along with the Christmas tree lights. Maybe they were for more than just looks.

Down at the hospital, Dr. Morgan paced his office floor, pausing now and then to stop and look anxiously out the window. How would Amy handle the coming storm? He knew he shouldn't fret, but he couldn't help it. "If anything bothers her and they need me, there's no way I'd be able to make it up to the cabin in the middle of a blizzard." He spoke the words half aloud.

"What was that?" Dr. Wright asked, pausing before Dr. Morgan's open door. "Were you talking to me,

Morgan?"

Justin turned around. "No, I was talking to myself."

Dr. Wright leaned against the doorframe. "Would it help to talk to someone else instead of just yourself?"

"I've got a feeling that I can't shake. It seems totally irrational when I think about it, but it continues to persist."

"What?"

"There's a severe winter storm moving our way, and if it's as bad as the weathermen on the radio are predicting, no one is going to be going to or from my parent's cabin for days possibly." Dr. Morgan stopped pacing to grip the back of his chair. "I'd have to leave soon if I am going to go up there."

"Why do you want to go up there?" Dr. Wright probed.

"Amy. I've got a feeling that . . . Well, that she might not take this storm too well. I told you the feeling was crazy, but—"

"I'd follow that feeling, Morgan. If something were to happen up there during the storm and you couldn't get there, it might send Amy back to the hospital. Douglas, Hollend and I can handle things here. So, get your coat and get going."

For a brief moment, Dr. Justin Morgan remained staring down at his desk. Then, snatching up his coat, he crossed the room to the door and held out his hand. "Thanks."

Returning the handshake, Dr. Wright nodded. "Just let us know that you made it there safely."

"Will do." Dr. Morgan's long strides carried him quickly down the hall, through the lobby, and out into the bitterly cold afternoon.

By the time supper was ready in the Morgan cabin, it had begun to snow and the subdued sound of the wind could be heard through the windows. Amy felt herself growing nervous. Was there something to be worried about? No one else seemed bothered. Drawing a long breath, she forced herself to concentrate on what was being said. She didn't feel hungry, but sat toying with the food on her plate.

"Amy," Mrs. Morgan asked, noticing the girl's untouched supper. "Aren't you hungry?"

"No, I guess not." She shivered as a stronger gust of wind rattled the window. How long was this storm going to last?

Suddenly, Captain, who was staying in the garage until the storm was over, started barking. Then the front door slammed against the wall and the sound of someone stomping in the hall was heard. Glances were exchanged and Mr. Morgan, placing his napkin on the table, rose. As he stepped into the living room, the others heard Justin's voice.

"Hi, Dad. It sure is shaping up to be some storm. Is your phone line still working?"

"Last I checked it was, but what are you doing up here in this weather?"

"I'll use the phone in the office. Be right back." His footsteps faded down the far hall and Mr. Morgan came back into the dining room.

"Better set another place, Sara," he said. "I doubt he's eaten."

When Justin joined the family a few minutes later, he slipped into the empty chair next to Sara and remarked, as though he hadn't just appeared unexpectedly in a storm,

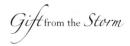

"It sure smells good. I'm hungry."

No one said a word. Even Sara simply looked at her brother.

Having filled his plate, Justin stabbed a bite and, as he lifted his fork, he found everyone gazing at him. With a sigh, he set his fork back down. "I suppose I can't eat until I've explained why I'm here. It's quite simple really. I had a strong urge to come up and Wright told me to do it. So here I am." He lifted his fork again.

"And the phone call?" Adam eyed his brother from across the table.

"To let Wright know I was here. You ought to see how it's coming down! And that wind—" He shook his head and returned to his supper.

It was obvious to the rest of the Morgan family that something more than just a "strong urge" had brought Justin up the mountain and into the storm. But they also knew that until he was ready to talk, they wouldn't get a thing out of him.

Justin's coming had distracted Amy enough so that she was able to eat some of her supper and help with the dishes. Her nervousness subsided or was at least forgotten for the time.

The evening hymns had been sung, with Justin agreeing to play the piano, and then Sara left to take Danny and Jenny up to bed.

"What a night," Adam remarked, putting another log on the fire and pausing to listen to the wind whistling around the chimney. "Have you looked outside lately?"

"Not since I got here," Justin replied, as no one else answered. "It was coming down hard enough then."

Amy shivered and rubbed her hands over her arms.

Biting her lower lip, she shifted her position. That sound was terrible! She could feel a tightness in her chest. Maybe if she walked she would feel better. Standing up, she moved across the room.

Then a particularly strong gust swept over the house, making a wild moaning in the chimney, and Amy gasped. Whirling around, her eyes wide with terror, she clutched the edge of the piano for support as dizziness swept over her.

"Amy, are you all right? Here, come over to the couch and sit down." Justin placed a hand on Amy's arm.

"No!" Amy jerked away and backed up. Her breathing was rapid and her whole body trembled. "No!" she said again.

Mrs. Morgan swiftly crossed the room to Amy's side. "Come with me, Dear. Everything is going to be all right," she soothed. "There is no need to be frightened. It is just the wind."

For a moment it looked as though Amy would allow herself to be drawn to the couch, but the rattling of the windows was too much. With a slight cry, Amy turned and fled across the room, crouching near the doorway.

~ 19 ~

"I was afraid of something like this," Justin remarked quietly, his eyes still on the terrified girl. "She's panicked. Where's Sara?"

"Still upstairs. Do you want her?" Mrs. Morgan wasn't sure what Sara could do to help Amy, but Justin should know what he was doing.

He nodded and slowly began crossing the room. "Amy." His voice was gentle and low. "It's going to be all right. You are safe now. You are not alone. Remember Christ's promise? 'I will never leave you nor forsake you.' Rest in that promise now, Amy."

Whimpering, Amy remained crouched by the wall. She heard Justin's words, but something, some large, terrifying "thing" seemed to hold her in its paralyzing grip, and she couldn't get free. With each roar of wind, each rattle of the window, each whistle in the chimney, the nameless terror pressed closer about her. She could hardly breathe! Wasn't there any way of escape?

"'Lo, I am with you always.' He hasn't left you, Amy." Justin dropped down beside her. "Adam, bring a glass of water, please. And my bag. It's in Dad's office." The low, soothing tone of his voice didn't change at his request, but

Adam heard and quickly disappeared.

Mrs. Morgan and Sara came into the living room. "What can I do, Just?" Sara asked, her eyes troubled at the sight of Amy.

With a motion of his head, Justin replied, "Go play the evening hymns. I think they might help."

As the strains of the first song sounded from the piano, Amy felt some of the tightness that had been about her chest, pressing the air from her lungs, loosen. She heard Justin talking and then felt his hand on her arm, helping her stand up. Her knees felt weak and she was glad of a strong arm to lean on. Her head ached. Sinking down onto the couch, she leaned back and closed her eyes.

Someone sat down beside her and Mrs. Morgan spoke softly, gently smoothing Amy's hair from her face, "It's all right now, Dear. Just relax."

A blanket was tucked over her lap and Amy felt a work hardened hand gently press her own. She knew it was Mr. Morgan though he said not a word.

"Here, Justin." It was Adam's calm, quiet voice. Maybe things were going to be all right.

Justin took his bag and pulled out a small bottle from which he poured a few drops into the glass of water. After replacing the bottle, he held the glass to Amy's lips. "Drink some of this, Amy."

Slowly Amy opened her eyes. Obediently she took a swallow and then reached for the glass. Her hands shook some, but she held on to it, staring at the tiny waves the water made. A memory, an image, faint but real, flickered through her mind. *Waves washing up on a beach. It was so peaceful, so calm . . .*

Into the midst of the quiet came the sudden, angry roar of the wind, a howl and whistle in the chimney, a snapping sound and then sudden darkness save for the fire's glow. Sara's hands crashed on a discord and then silence. Gripping the glass in her hands, Amy froze, her heart pounding in her chest; they were going to crash! With a scream, she sprang up, her hands clenching the glass until it shattered as she struggled to escape the folds of the blanket.

"Amy!"

Hands tried to hold her, but Amy was frantic and fought them off. She didn't know where she was going, but she had to get away. Where were the children? "Danny! Jenny!" Her voice choked over a sob. No, she couldn't do this, she couldn't! Stumbling over a stool, she fell against the stone chimney. It was solid, it felt secure. She clutched it and cried, sweat trickled down her face and her whole body trembled. Would this nightmare never end?

A light, dim at first then brighter, came from the lamps; voices were beside her. She could hear them talking.

"Sara, play! Dad, Adam, keep her still if you can. Be careful of that glass!"

"Justin, her hands are bleeding!"

"I know, Mother. That's next."

Amy felt her sleeve being pushed up and then the sharp prick of something. A song, her favorite evening hymn was being sung. Was that Sara's voice? It was sweeter than before. She was tired and she leaned against a strong arm. "I want to go to bed," she whimpered. "I want out. I want out."

"Adam, help me move the other couch over. Mother, can you get another blanket? This one has glass all over it." Justin spoke quietly but with an efficiency that got things done. Soon the other couch was moved near the fire and Amy was carried over. A pillow was placed under her head and a blanket was tucked around her.

"Warm water, Mother, please. Dad, I need more light." Justin sat down beside his patient and, after checking her pulse, gently turned her hands over. The sharp edges from the shattered glass had cut her hands and fingers. With the added light of a flashlight which his dad held, Justin was able to see well enough to remove a few splinters of glass before carefully washing the wounded hands.

"Adam, you're bleeding," Mrs. Morgan exclaimed softly.

Justin looked up. "I'll look at it in a minute," he said, noticing the blood stains on his brother's rolled-up shirtsleeve and his upper arm.

But Adam shrugged. "It's nothing really. Just a scratch. I'll go wash it off and change shirts."

"Better let me look at it if it came from the water glass," Justin told him. "There could be glass splinters in it."

Amy moaned and moved restlessly as Justin finished binding her hands. "Easy, Amy," he soothed. "Just relax. Nothing is going to hurt you."

Her eyes opened and she looked around in an uneasy, half troubled way. Catching sight of Mr. Morgan, she reached out a hand. "Dad, pray, please!" Tears gathered in her eyes and trickled down her cheeks. "I'm scared and I don't know why!"

Mr. Morgan took the injured hand tenderly. The piano softened, Mrs. Morgan gently stroked Amy's light hair as Adam stood by ready to do anything and Justin watched the girl's face keenly. The prayer seemed to quiet

Amy even more and when it was over she lay still, her eyes closed and her breathing growing steadier. Only after Justin was sure Amy was asleep did he turn his attention to his brother's injured arm.

"Did she hit you with the glass?" he asked, pulling a sliver from the deepest cut.

"I don't know. It all happened so quickly." Adam winced slightly.

"How did she break the glass?" Sara asked, looking across the room from the piano.

Dressing the wound, Justin replied, "I think she crushed it with her hands. It was probably a compulsive movement and she didn't even realize it." He turned and eyed Amy carefully. Stepping over, he placed fingers lightly on her pulse. It was steadier.

Everyone was subdued by the events which had just taken place and, though they had many questions, no one felt like talking about it yet. The glass was swept up, the blanket taken away and the water wiped up. Another log was placed on the fire and Adam put on his flannel shirt which he had taken off to romp with Danny.

At last Sara voiced a question. "Is she going to sleep in her room tonight?"

Slowly Justin shook his head. "No, I think it's too far away from everyone. She could . . ." He paused as another strong gust of wind whistled and roared down the chimney and Amy whimpered and moved restlessly. "I think she would be better in some place where the sound of the wind isn't so noticeable. For some reason she seems greatly bothered by it."

"What about upstairs, Son," Mrs. Morgan suggested. "The chimney isn't near the girls' room. She could sleep in

Heather's old bed."

"It would also be warmer up there since the power is out," Mr. Morgan added. "At least for a time. We may all have to camp out here near the fireplace if the storm keeps up many days."

"Sound good. Let's wait a little while longer though. Will you keep playing, Sare?"

Sara nodded and, playing a few chords to change keys, she began Amy's favorite evening hymn. Her sweet soprano took up the words and the rest of the family joined in.

"God, that madest earth and heaven,
Darkness and light;
Who the day for toil hast given,
For rest the night;
May Thy angel guards defend us,
Slumber sweet Thy mercy send us;
Holy dreams and hopes attend us
This live-long night."

It was late, nearly midnight, yet beside the fire sat Mr. Morgan with his two sons. Amy was asleep upstairs in the girls' room, with Sara in the bed beside her and Mrs. Morgan within call.

"Justin, you never told us why you came up here this evening?" Mr. Morgan looked over at his son.

"To tell you the truth, Dad, I was worried." He looked up, his face grave in the firelight, his arms resting on his knees as he leaned forward. "I couldn't get away from the feeling that Amy might have a reaction to the storm. I mentioned it to Wright and he said to come up."

"I'm glad you did," Mr. Morgan sighed with a shake of his head. "I don't know what we would have done."

"Justin, why do you think she reacted that way?"

Justin turned to look at his brother. "It's hard to tell for sure, but I'd guess the sounds of the wind reminded her of whatever it was that sent her and the children wandering in the mountains. I could be wrong. I suppose it could be something farther back in her past."

Adam frowned in thought. "What would make that sound?" he mused. "A train? A wild animal?"

"What about a car losing control?" Mr. Morgan suggested.

"I suppose that could explain why the fire seemed to frighten her. The car or vehicle slid or something, the driver lost control, and when they crashed, the vehicle caught on fire." Justin paused. "But it just doesn't seem right. Surely, if it was a car, someone would have spotted the wreck and all Amy would have had to do was get back on the road with the children."

"I agree. Dad, are there any trains that go through these mountains?"

Rubbing his chin, Mr. Morgan pursed his lips. "I can't think of any . . . But, I do have an old map with all the old railroads for these mountains. Why don't we get it out and take a look." He stood up. "I'll bring it out here, since the lights are out."

He returned moments later and he and Adam bent over it for some minutes.

"Hey, Dad," Justin said, a puzzled look on his face. "If it was a train wreck, everyone would know about it and there would be a passenger list. Besides, Amy hasn't seemed affected at all by Danny's train."

For some time the three men sat trying to think and coming up with nothing. No matter what they thought of, there were objections. If it was a commercial vehicle, wouldn't someone know it had never arrived? If it was a private car, the wreck would have been discovered. Had there been any other avalanches? Could they have been in a cabin? To each and every question they reached the same conclusion; It might be, but probably not.

Suddenly Adam sat up straight. "A storm! Maybe it wasn't a vehicle at all."

~20~

"Huh?" Justin's train of thought had been jolted by his brother's exclamation and it took him a minute to focus again. "What do you mean?"

"We haven't thought about a storm in connection with Amy's experience. But weren't there a lot of storms in the mountains days before she arrived?"

Justin shook his head. "I don't remember. What if there were?"

"What if they were camping or hiking and got lost in the mountains?"

"That would explain why she was terrified of the wind," Mr. Morgan noted with a nod.

"But how do you explain what she had to get the children out of?" Justin queried. "She said it was something dark or bad."

"It could have been a cabin; maybe it was struck by lightning. She takes the children out and gets lost."

"Could be. But did they live there? Who are Danny and Jenny's parents? Why has no one searched for them? That's what's starting to really trouble me."

"Hmm, maybe a storm happened while they were lost. You know what a mountain storm can be like."

"So—" Justin shifted in his chair and stared at his brother without really seeing him. "They could have been hiking, gotten lost and then a storm came up." He nodded slowly. "That might be it. But where did they come from?"

It was Adam's turn to shake his head.

Mr. Morgan tapped his fingers on the arm of his chair and crossed a foot over his other knee. "She could be out of state. Perhaps she stopped somewhere to let the kids run and then got lost. If that's the case, the parents of Danny and Jenny could be anywhere."

"Then why would Amy have the children?" Justin rubbed his hand across his forehead.

No one had an answer and Mr. Morgan glanced from one son to another. "Maybe we are trying too hard. It is late and we're all tired. Perhaps—"

The clock, striking one-thirty, interrupted.

"Let's call it a night," Justin suggested.

"I agree." And Adam carefully banked the fire.

When morning came, it was still dark and the storm still raged. Everyone was thankful for the oil lamps providing some light. Amy, exhausted by the panic of the day before and still nervous and apprehensive, refused to remain in a room alone.

"I can't explain how I feel," she told Justin with troubled eyes. "I think I'm going to scream if I have to listen to that wind much longer."

"Do you think music would help?" he asked. "I can't make the wind stop, but perhaps some piano playing would help block the sound." He rose as he spoke and crossed to the piano, Amy following. "Now, what would you like?" he asked, sitting down and running his fingers up and down the keys. He looked up with a smile.

"I don't know. Not something sad."

After striking a chord here and there, as he thought, Justin suddenly started in on a lively tune which sent Amy's toes to tapping. The rest of the Morgan family, drawn by the music, soon joined the two around the piano. Sara slid onto the bench beside her brother and he, without missing a beat, made room for her. Together they made the room alive with waltzes, marches, polkas and rousing folk songs from their childhood.

At last Justin made one final chord and stopped. "Whew, that's the longest I've played at one sitting for quite a while. I'm tired!"

Sara agreed. "Those last two songs were terrible. I couldn't seem to find the right notes at all!"

"So I noticed," Justin laughed, standing up and stretching. "Mother, would we be permitted to make fudge?"

"Fudge!" Sara squealed, not giving her mother a chance to say a word. "Let's go. We'll make two kinds. Adam and Justin, we'll need you to stir them after you bring wood for the wood stove. Come on, Amy!"

Before following Sara, Justin looked down at his mother questioningly. "Well?"

Mrs. Morgan laughed. "I don't mind. Just don't spoil your appetite for lunch," she called after the forms already arriving in the kitchen where the sound of banging pots and pans was heard.

Between the efforts of the older Morgan children, their parents, and Danny and Jenny, Amy managed to make it through the day without becoming overwhelmed or hysterical by the feelings of fear which still haunted her at the raging of the storm. There were many prayers that day sent up for and from the troubled girl.

By late evening the wind had died down and the snow had stopped falling. Everything was quiet, but the house was chilly. The family sat around the fireplace with sweaters on.

"Amy, you can't sleep in your room tonight," Mrs. Morgan said after the evening hymns had been sung. "It's much too cold. Spend the night in Sara's room again until the men get the power back on."

Sara was delighted at the idea. "We'll have a slumber party, and we can talk all night if we want to."

The two girls departed and Amy's voice came floating down from the walkway. "But how can we talk and slumber at the same time?"

The following morning Amy watched as Sara donned warm winter clothes, grabbed a shovel, and went out to help her dad and brothers begin the long hard work of shoveling themselves out. Captain, delighted to be free from his imprisonment in the garage, barked and wallowed his way to the porch where he followed the shovelers, poking his nose into the drifts of snow and barking.

With delighted interest, Danny and Jenny watched out the window and shouted when anyone threw a snowball at them. For a time, Amy watched also, then tiring, she curled up in a chair and closed her eyes. A feeling of exhaustion swept over her and she sighed. It was going to be a long winter if there were many more such storms as they had just had. She wasn't sure she could stand another one.

Though the storm was over and the sun broke through the clouds around mid-morning, the Morgan cabin was growing colder and all were thankful for the fireplace. With the house chilly, everyone tried to remain near the bright blaze or in the kitchen where their wood burning stove still allowed hot meals to be prepared. "You know, Amy," Mrs. Morgan had told her that morning, "the children all tried to talk me into getting rid of this old stove when I got a new electric one, but I insisted it stay. And it's a mighty good thing I did too." Amy heartily agreed. Not only could they eat hot meals, but they had even made their fudge on it the day before.

"I feel like Laura Ingalls Wilder in the "Little House" books," Amy confided to Sara as they waited for the water to heat to wash the dishes. "This is much more interesting than a regular stove."

"And a lot more work." Sara lifted the kettle and poured the hot water into the sink. "Here's the water, Mary. I'll wipe. I suppose Pa's out milkin' the cow."

Amy laughed. It was the first real, free laugh she had given since the storm had begun. "Yep. Laura, did you gather the eggs?"

"Oh, I forgot! I was too busy fishing."

Adam stepped into the kitchen with more wood for the stove, but paused at Sara's words. "Fishing?" he asked with raised eyebrows.

Amy and Sara looked at each other with suppressed smiles. "Just put the wood in the wood box and go do your other chores, Almonzo," Amy directed with a giggle. "I'm sure Pa and Royal are needing your help."

"And gather the eggs, too," Sara added.

Adam eyed both girls and shook his head.

No sooner had he disappeared into the hall than Sara and Amy burst into a hearty laugh.

It felt good to laugh and enjoy living again, Amy thought. The sky was full of stars and the men, with help from Sara, had made good progress towards reaching the main road. Perhaps she could help shovel some tomorrow. It looked like fun.

Late the following afternoon the snowplows reached their driveway and soon after, Justin drove back down to town and the hospital. It was another few days before the electric lines were repaired and heat and lights returned to the Morgan cabin.

* * *

Dr. Morgan stepped from a patient's room and strode quickly down the hall. Glancing at his watch he noticed the time. "One more patient to see and then a few papers to finish filling out and I'll be off duty."

He knocked softly at the next door and a voice called, "Come in."

"Good evening, Taylor," Dr. Morgan greeted his patient. "How's the arm feeling?"

The reply became a murmur as the door was shut behind the doctor.

A quarter of an hour later, the door opened and Dr. Morgan paused and looked back into the room. "Oh, I'll let you go in a day or so, but you'll have to promise me you'll try not to crash your sled again." He gave a chuckle and wished Taylor good-night.

Upon seeing Philips in the lobby, Dr. Morgan stopped for a few words with him before continuing to his office where a visitor was waiting.

"Adam! What are you doing here? Is everything all

right at the cabin?" Dr. Morgan's face held a look of concern at the sight of his brother.

"Everything is fine. But I wanted to talk to you. When are you off?"

"As soon as I get a few papers finished. They shouldn't take me more than ten minutes or so." He pulled out his chair and sat down. "Are you sure things are all right?"

Adam nodded. "Everything is fine. Just get those papers finished. I want to talk."

Dr. Justin Morgan pulled a couple of files closer and opened the first one. Why had Adam come to talk? Something had to be going on. He looked up. "Adam, what—"

"Would you get busy?" Adam looked exasperated. "If you don't hurry up, I'll go talk to Dr. Wright!"

"I won't say another word."

The papers took longer than Justin had hoped, partly because his brain was having trouble focusing. At last they were finished and he closed the last folder. "Done. Now, are we talking here?"

Adam shrugged. "Wherever."

"Then let's go to my place."

The walk to the boarding house was taken in silence and it wasn't until both brothers were seated in Justin's small set of rooms that Adam began.

"I got a phone call early this morning from the police in Jackson."

Justin froze, a steaming cup of coffee half way to his lips. "What?"

Choosing to ignore the question, Adam continued. "They wanted to talk and asked me to bring pictures of

Amy and the children. Dad and I both went." He paused and looked at his brother. Justin hadn't moved. "They made contact with some neighbors of the couple who had died in the avalanche and were told that they had taken in an older girl and her two younger siblings until arrangements could be finalized to get them to their relatives in Florida or some southern state. They didn't know if the three siblings had gone to their relatives or not. If not, they weren't sure what became of them. But," he added, "they said one of the children was called Danny."

There was a soft thud as Justin's coffee cup was returned to the table with not a drop tasted. Though his mouth opened, Justin couldn't think of a word to say.

"The police are sending copies of the pictures to the police in—I forgot the name of where the couple was from. The neighbors might be able to identify them."

It took several tries before Justin was able to talk. His mouth seemed to suddenly go dry. "Where's Dad?"

"Gone back home. He had to get something to Mother he picked up."

"Then she might have relatives."

"Who? Mother?" Adam stared at his brother.

"No, Amy." He shook his head. "Sorry, my brain is spinning. So, you are saying that if Amy and the children are who the neighbors say they might be, then they are all siblings and they have relatives in some southern state?"

Adam nodded. "Yep."

"Are the Jackson police going to let you know when they hear anything?"

"Uh huh."

"The neighbors didn't know anyone's name but Danny?"

Adam shook his head. "Nope." He seemed to have

used most of his words in telling the news and now only had monosyllables left.

Absentmindedly Justin fingered the handle on his cup. "And if they aren't the right ones, could the parents have gotten lost too?"

"Huh?"

"Danny and Jenny's parents. If they aren't the right people, I mean, the ones those neighbors think—I'm getting confused myself—then perhaps the parents were lost in the mountains with the others and became separated. Did Dad check for any other lost people?"

"Yes. That's one of the first things he did besides put out notices."

"But they didn't find anyone."

"No."

"Well." Justin picked up his cup and took a drink. "Ugh, this is cold." He shoved the cold coffee away from him. "Did you say Dad went back home? How are you planning on getting home then?"

"I was hoping you'd let me stay here—"

Knock, knock.

Rebekah A. Morris

~*21*~

Justin rose to answer the door, saying over his shoulder, "Sure you can stay here, if you don't mind sleeping on the couch." He opened the door. "Why, Wright, what brings you here? Come in. I'd invite you to stay for supper, but Adam hasn't fixed any yet."

Dr. Alex Wright stepped in and rubbed his hands. "I didn't know Adam was your new cook," he laughed.

"Neither did I!" Adam rose and held out his hand. Dr. Wright was a friend of the whole Morgan family. He had gone to medical school with Justin and had often been brought home for the holidays since his family was traveling in Europe. When Justin had begun to plan for the hospital, Wright was the first doctor he had talked with.

"Take off your coat and stay a while," Justin offered. "We'll fill you in on the continuing mystery of who Amy is."

"That sounds interesting, but I'm afraid you'll have to miss it."

Justin looked puzzled. "I'll have to miss it? Why?"

"Because Mrs. Duffey insists that you must visit her right away as her ankle is 'hurting something fierce.' She called to me as I was passing her house. I offered to check it, but no, she declared she 'didn't believe in having more than one doctor attending a person. It just made things worse'." Dr. Wright grinned as Justin groaned. "I didn't argue."

"I suppose I must go and see her. But why didn't she use the telephone instead of shouting at you?"

"Because she was sweeping off her front porch."

"Alex, she wasn't!" Dr. Morgan stared unbelievingly at his friend.

Dr. Wright nodded. "She was."

"That woman!" Justin muttered, jerking on his coat and snatching up his medical bag. "I told her to stay off of that leg unless it was absolutely necessary!" Stepping outside, he pulled the door shut with a little more force than was needed.

With head bent against a brisk breeze, Justin made his way along the sidewalk until he arrived at the modest home of Mrs. Duffey, her married son and his wife. Justin knew the son traveled often. Mounting the porch, he pressed the doorbell and heard the muffled sound of chimes.

The door opened almost at once and the younger Mrs. Duffey appeared, looking quite relieved when she saw who it was. "Thank goodness you came, Doctor," she said in low tones, stepping aside so Justin could enter the hallway. "I don't know what to do with her. She has been on her feet most of the day and," she glanced cautiously down the hall, "insists that everything was necessary."

"Clara," a voice called from the other room, "is that Dr. Morgan?"

"Yes, Mother."

"Well, show him in here."

Clara Duffey looked at Dr. Morgan helplessly and shrugged. "She won't listen to me."

"Me either, it seems." And Dr. Morgan stepped down the hall and entered the parlor where Mrs. Duffey sat in a rocker with her feet on a footstool.

"Come right in, Dr. Morgan," called Mrs. Duffey waving a hand to a nearby chair. "I would have called you on the telephone, but I do hate to use them things because that girl down at the switchboard can listen in to everything I say. It was a good thing that other doctor was passing the house. Come, come. Sit down. My ankle is terrible painful." Leaning back in her chair, she placed a hand near her throat and took several quick breaths.

Setting down his bag on one chair and drawing another near the footstool, Dr. Morgan waited until his patient had finished talking. "What is this I hear about you disobeying my orders and sweeping the front porch?" His face was grave.

"You said I could get up, Doctor."

"I said only if it was necessary. Sweeping off your porch wasn't."

Mrs. Duffey uttered a faint moan as her shoe was removed. "It was necessary, Doctor. Johnny is coming home this evening and I didn't want him slipping on the snow. And Clara was busy doing other things," she added before he could say anything.

Dr. Morgan didn't look up from the injured limb. "What else have you been doing today? You must have been on your feet quite a bit for your ankle to be in this state."

"Well, I did a few things, but only what was necessary. Clara is such a young thing, you know, and can't be expected to run a house by herself." Mrs. Duffey shrugged. "Clara!"

Young Mrs. Duffey stuck her head in the door. "Yes, Mother?"

"Bring me a cup of tea, won't you? Would you like any, Doctor?"

"No thank you."

Clara withdrew her head and Mrs. Duffey continued talking. "The dusting, you know, just had to be done. Clara never wants to move each thing and dust under it. She says things only need dusted once a week. Can you imagine? Oh!" The exclamation was involuntary.

Dr. Morgan looked up. "Does it hurt?"

"Dreadfully, Doctor," and Mrs. Duffey closed her eyes and fanned herself with her hand. "But I know you can make it feel better. You are such a good doctor," she murmured.

A long silence followed. Realizing that his patient must be really suffering since she hadn't said a word for two minutes, Dr. Morgan said, "I'm going to go get some water to bathe your ankle. It is quite swollen."

"Clara can fetch it," Mrs. Duffey opened her eyes to say. "Cla—"

"No." Dr. Morgan's decisive interruption cut the name off in the middle. He rose. "Your daughter-in-law has done quite enough for today and should take a rest. I'll be right back. Don't move from that chair!"

Quietly he left the parlor and walked down the hall to the kitchen. He wondered if John Duffey would come home before he left. "There are a few things I'd like to talk to him about," he thought.

The kitchen door was open and as Justin stepped in, he saw Mrs. Clara Duffey seated at the table, her head in her hands. The kettle whistled on the stove but she made no move. With two quick steps, Justin crossed the kitchen and lifted the tea kettle, pouring hot water over the tea leaves into the teapot which stood waiting on the counter. After setting the kettle on a cool part of the stove, he turned to the woman at the table. "Mrs. Duffey."

There was no response.

"Clara." He touched her shoulder and she jerked her head up.

"What? Oh, I'm sorry. I must have dozed off. Does Mother need me? Her tea. I forgot about it." She started to rise, but Dr. Morgan gently pushed her back.

"The tea is steeping. Are you all right?"

She sighed. "Yes. I'm more tired these days than I used to be."

"That's to be expected. But I think you might be overdoing it in your condition."

Mrs. Clara looked up, puzzled. "My condition? I don't know what you mean, Doctor. Are you talking about Mother?"

"No, I'm talking about you. When is your baby due?"

"Baby? I'm not having a baby, Doctor. Though goodness knows, John and I have wanted one for years. But the doctors in Jackson said we couldn't have children."

Justin had filled a basin with cool water and now set it on the table. "Have you talked with Dr. Hollend over at the hospital?"

Mrs. Clara shook her head and rose to pour a cup of tea for her mother-in-law.

"I think you should see him. I don't have as much experience as he does when it comes to babies, but I think—"

"Clara!" the shrill voice of Mrs. Duffey echoed down the hall from the parlor.

"Mother is waiting for her tea," was all Mrs. Clara said as she picked up the steaming cup.

With a troubled frown, Justin followed with the basin of water. He would have to have that talk with John. He couldn't think about it much though for, as he approached the parlor, he could hear Mrs. Duffey talking.

"Clara, fetch that afghan from over there, won't you? Now I'll take that cup of tea. I do hope you have made it strong the way I like it." A momentary pause as the tea was tasted. "It's not bad, but it could have used a longer steaming time. Young people can't be expected to make a proper cup of tea, I suppose. Doctor, I must confess that I don't approve of your leaving for such a length of time. Clara could have fetched the water. Clara," she turned her attention to her daughter-in-law who was looking out the front window. "Clara, what are you staring at?"

"Nothing, Mother." And Clara turned.

"Have you started supper?"

"Not yet."

"I'm surprised at you, Clara! Johnny will be coming home soon. You'd best get started. If it weren't for this ankle of mine, I'd go do it myself. Doctor, if you'll just help me into the kitchen I can at least peel potatoes. Come, help me up." Throwing off her afghan, Mrs. Duffey placed one foot on the floor and motioned with her hand.

Justin saw Clara's pale, tired face. "I'm afraid your supper will just have to wait," he said quietly. "Mrs. Duffey, you are not to stir from that chair. And your daughter is going to sit down in this rocker and put her feet up." He spoke decidedly and rose to place a footstool before the rocker for the younger Mrs. Duffey. "You both have been up and about too much today."

After Mrs. Clara had, without a word, dropped down

in the rocker he had pointed to, Dr. Morgan took a light blanket and spread it over her knees. "Just sit and relax," he told her quietly. Then he resumed his seat before his first patient and began bathing the ankle without a word.

"Well, I never!" ejaculated Mrs. Duffey after a full five minutes of silence. "Someone must get supper."

"Well, it won't be either of you," was the decided answer. "You are both under my orders for the time."

Mrs. Duffey finished her cup of tea and set it on the nearby table with considerable rattling. "But . . . but . . ." she spluttered, "Clara isn't sick, Doctor."

Justin refused to answer, but kept his eyes on his work. He knew Mrs. Duffey loved to argue and he wasn't going to aid her in it.

Heavy steps sounded on the porch and then the door creaked open and the screen door slammed.

"Johnny!" Mrs. Duffey, called. "Is that you?"

"Yes, Mother." A hearty voice answered, and the thud of the front door shook the pictures on the wall.

Mrs. Duffey shook her head. "That boy. He's always slamming doors."

"Hi, Mother. Doctor, what are you doing here? I thought Clara told me Mother's ankle was doing fine?"

Justin looked up. "It was until she decided to disregard orders and use it most of the day."

"The things I did were necessary," Mrs. Duffey insisted.

"Sweeping the snow off the porch was not necessary," Dr. Morgan stated.

"I should say not!" John Duffey agreed heartily, shaking hands with Justin. "I'm glad you could come over, Doctor." Glancing around, John caught sight of his wife's eager face. "Hello, Honey!" His long legs almost tripped on a chair as he hurried to greet his wife. "Miss me?"

Clara's answer was too low to understand and Justin didn't try.

"Say, what are you sitting here for at this time of day? You're not sick, are you?" There was alarm in his tones and he placed a hand on her forehead.

"No, I'm only tired."

"It is Doctor Morgan's fault you have no supper tonight, Johnny," Mrs. Duffey said. She was a bit put out with the young doctor for issuing orders so freely in her house.

Skillfully fitting a bandage on the injured ankle, Justin didn't look up as he replied, "Yep, I'll take all the blame. I've given orders that these two ladies are to remain in their chairs for the time being. There you are, Mrs. Duffey." He seized a nearby pillow and placed it on top of the footstool to give the ankle a softer place to rest. "Now, I don't want you using that ankle at all until I give you leave!" He stood up. "John, if she doesn't stay off that ankle, give me a call. I can arrange for her to stay at the hospital until it is well enough to use."

John turned. "I'll see to it that she follows orders, Doctor. I don't have to go anywhere for several weeks."

"I won't go to any hospital," Mrs. Duffey fussed. "I never did like those smelly places."

"Then stay off that foot! Now, could I have a few words with you, John?" Dr. Morgan picked up the basin of water and nodded to the other room.

When they were alone in the kitchen, Justin started. "I want you to take your wife to the hospital tomorrow morning and have Dr. Hollend examine her."

John staggered against the wall and stared, his face

registering alarm. "Why? She said she wasn't sick!"

"I don't think she is sick."

"But you just said—"

"I said Dr. Hollend should examine her. John, I think you are going to be welcoming a baby into your house before many more weeks."

"You—what?" John sank into the nearest chair. "You . . . you're sure?"

"I can't be positive without an examination, but she's either going to have a baby or she's sick. Either way, she should see a doctor. And," Justin added, "she shouldn't be doing as much work as she has been."

"Doctor, can't you do it?"

"I'm afraid I'm not very good at dusting," Justin replied dryly.

This seemed to bring John out of his shocked state for he shook his head. "I don't mean her work, I can do that. I mean find out if she's having . . . I mean . . . if we knew. The docs in Jackson said we couldn't have a baby. But . . ." His pleading gaze was fixed on Justin's face. "Please Doc! Just let us know if—I won't sleep a wink if I have to wait. And I don't want to tell Mother because she'd be up and doing, ankle or no ankle, and . . . well, she's bound to get it out of me if I have to wait. Please, Doc!"

Justin had never been as interested in taking care of mothers and babies as he had in fixing broken bones and dealing with sickness. That was why Dr. Hollend had been added to the team. He decided to try a compromise. "I'll agree to do a quick exam if you'll promise to take Clara to Dr. Hollend first thing tomorrow morning."

"I'll agree to anything if you only will!"

~22~

Arriving back at his home, Justin found Dr. Wright and Adam seated at the table littered with nearly empty dishes. "I was beginning to think Mrs. Duffey had you locked up in a closet," Wright teased. "Was she that difficult?"

Justin smiled, slid off his coat and went to the sink to wash up. "She was difficult, but that's not what took me so long."

He came back to the table and Adam handed him a plate of hot food.

"Well?"

"An unexpected arrival is due, I'm guessing in five or six weeks."

"Who's coming?" Dr. Wright looked mildly interested. "I suppose Mrs. Duffey had to tell you all about it."

Swallowing the bite he had just taken, Justin shook his head. "Nope. To tell you the truth, she doesn't even know of the new arrival. We thought it best not to mention it to her with her ankle like it is."

Adam and Dr. Wright exchanged puzzled glances. What was Justin talking about? Reaching across the table,

Dr. Wright felt his friend's head and tried to take his pulse, but Justin pushed his hand aside.

"Oh, stop it. I'm not sick. But that reminds me, I need to call Hollend and tell him Mrs. Clara Duffey is coming to see him in the morning."

"A baby?" Wright stared for a moment and then grinned. "Won't Mrs. Duffey be something with a baby in the house. But you said unexpected. What do you mean?"

Justin shrugged. "No one knew. But to change the subject, did Adam fill you in on what he's learned from Jackson?"

The rest of the evening was spent going over every scrap of information about Amy and the two children, and it was late before Dr. Wright left for his own boarding house leaving the brothers to get some sleep.

* * *

Days and then weeks passed. Amy and Sara both grew tired of the constant snow and longed for the warmer breath of spring. Even the distractions in town with Mrs. Clara Duffey's new baby, visiting Heather and the children or going shopping were getting old.

"Let's stop by the hospital and see Justin before we go back home," Sara suggested after she and Amy had spent the morning shopping.

"Won't he be busy?" Amy inquired.

Sara shrugged. "Perhaps. But he might not be."

Stepping into the old hotel lobby, Amy gazed at the gilt and trim. She didn't remember noticing it the day she left the hospital. It was quite lovely, and the staircase looked like—what did it remind her of? A puzzled frown crossed her face and she stared into space. What was it?

Why did this staircase bring back a flash of a similar one?

"Amy?" Sara touched her arm. "Are you all right?"

"That stairway . . . I think . . . No, I don't think. I can't. But I saw it just a minute ago when we walked in."

"Saw what?" Sara watched her friend's face with sympathy.

"Another staircase almost like this, but I . . . I don't know where it was!" She groaned and shook her head. "Maybe I should never go anywhere."

"That doesn't sound very pleasant." A new voice spoke beside the girls and they turned to see Dr. Wright smiling at them. "I'd get cabin fever if I was stuck in one place all the time.

"I would too!" Sara's emphatic answer brought a laugh. When it was over, she asked, "Do you know where Justin is?"

Dr. Wright nodded, "Yep, he's gone to make a call at one of the houses south of town. Do you need him? I'm not sure there's a phone to reach him there."

Sara shook her head. "No, not really. We were just looking for something else to do. We're both tired of the cabin and the snow and shopping and everything else we can think of." She gave a dismal sigh and sat down in one of the chairs nearby while Amy wandered across the room to look at a picture hanging on the wall.

Dr. Wright watched her walk away before saying in low tones to Sara, "How is she doing?"

"Fine most of the time. Now and then something seems to catch her off guard or startles her. Like when we walked in here. She stared at the staircase and said it reminded her of another one, but she didn't know where or what."

"How did she do in the storm we had last week? Justin was telling me about the blizzard." Dr. Wright leaned casually against the vacant receptionists desk and shoved one hand into the pocket of his white jacket.

"She didn't panic this time, but there were several times I thought she was going to. We did a lot of praying and singing while the storm lasted. They seem to be the only things which help. I don't think the snow bothers her, it's the sound of the wind." Sara shuddered. "I've never seen anyone look as terrified as Amy did the night of the blizzard. It was—" she shook her head, unable to explain it. "I wish Adam would hear back from Jackson."

"No word yet?"

"Nothing."

Amy turned back and came over to join them. "What are we going to do, Sara?"

With another long sigh, Sara rose. "I suppose we'll just go home. Maybe we'll think of something to do on the way." Both girls said good bye and headed back outside.

Neither one said anything until Sara was driving the car back up the mountain. "Sometimes, like today, I wish we lived in Florida!"

"Florida?"

Suddenly Sara remembered that the couple who had died in the avalanche might have taken Amy and the children in until they could go to their relatives in Florida or some other southern state. She glanced over at Amy, but no look of bewilderment was on her face. "Or maybe Louisiana, Georgia, South Carolina or some other southern state where they've never heard of snow."

Amy laughed. "If you lived there you'd probably be longing for a winter with snow."

"Probably." Sara lapsed into silence.

One snowy day followed another until at last Adam came in the cabin one morning and remarked, "Spring's coming."

Sara ceased the scales she had been practicing on the piano and Amy looked up from her knitting. "How do you know?" the former demanded eagerly.

"Smelled it. And I've seen two flocks of geese heading north."

"I want to smell it," Danny ran up to Adam. "Let me smell it too!"

"Me three!" Sara jumped up from the piano bench.

"Me four," Amy laughed, setting aside her knitting.

A voice called down from the walkway. "Where are you all going?"

Amy tipped her head. "To smell spring."

"Jenny and I will be right out with you." And Mrs. Morgan picked up the little girl and hurried for the stairs.

Amy waited for them and helped Jenny into her coat. "Let's go smell spring, Jenny Wren," she said, buttoning the small pink coat and kissing the round face inside the hood.

Not quite sure what it was all about, but eager to be a part of it, Jenny nodded. "Outside," she chuckled.

"Yes, spring is coming outside." Amy swung the little girl up onto her hip.

Once outside with the others, Amy looked around and sniffed. There was certainly a new smell in the air. Though the ground was still covered with snow, the sky above was a richer blue than Amy had seen for a long time. A light breeze blew and rustled the bare branches and whispered through the pines, caressing the cheeks of the small group gathered.

"That's a spring breeze all right," Mrs. Morgan remarked quietly. "I wouldn't be surprised if the first spring thaw happens soon."

"Then it'll be time to till and plant the garden." Adam gazed across the snowy landscape as though he could already see the freshly tilled earth.

Sara couldn't resist a chance to tease. "Go ahead. I want to watch you till the garden in the snow."

But Adam didn't do more than smile. He wasn't like Justin, and Sara had often complained to her younger brother in jest that he wasn't nearly as much fun as Justin.

To Amy, the prospect of spring brought mixed emotions. In one sense she was delighted at the thought of seeing green grass and flowers again, of hearing the birds sing in the trees and feeling a warm sun shining on her, but another part of her hesitated and held back, dreading the arrival of a new season. It had been many months since she had arrived at the Morgan home and still she couldn't remember anything. Would she ever get back the past life she had lost? Would she ever be able to know where those images which flashed through her mind at unexpected times belonged? Would she ever know who she was and where she came from?

A tug on her coat brought her mind back to the present. "Amy, come walk." Danny was gazing up at her, his voice insistent.

"All right." Amy shifted Jenny to the other arm and followed the young leader down the long driveway. "Where are we going?" she asked him.

"For a walk. We going to hunt bears." Peering all around him, Danny raised his hands. "There's one. Bang, bang. He's dead."

"Where did you get that idea?" Amy grinned.

"From my head. Do you see a bear?"

"Roar!" Sara charged from behind Amy and lunged for Danny who shrieked with delight and tried to run away. But Sara was too quick for him and snatched him up with another roar. "Here, Adam," she growled, "this hunter was trying to shoot us." Sara dumped the squealing boy into her brother's arms and reached for Jenny.

Clinging with both arms to Amy's neck, Jenny giggled.

"Perhaps we should go back inside," Amy suggested after a few more minutes of wild play. "It isn't spring yet."

Sara reluctantly agreed and challenged Danny to race her to the house. After they had dashed off, Adam took Jenny and set her on his shoulders.

"Are you feeling uneasy about spring?"

Amy turned at Adam's sudden question. How did he know what she had been thinking? "A little," she admitted. "I guess I'm afraid of changes right now. I want to remember, but I don't." She shook her head. "I feel so mixed up."

"I imagine anyone in your situation would feel that way. The question is, are you going to let it make you afraid of facing life or are you going to trust that your Heavenly Father knows what is best?"

Amy didn't reply. Often Adam's quiet, almost casual remarks left her thinking. He never seemed to expect an answer, but moved on and let his words do their own work.

It wasn't until they were inside taking their coats off, that Amy spoke again. "Thanks, Adam. I don't know if I have a younger brother, I don't think I do, but—well, if I had a choice, I'd want one like you."

Adam's quiet smile was all he answered.

Ring. Ring.

Rolling over in bed, Justin groped for the phone. "Hello?" he yawned. "Adam? What time is it? . . . Yeah, but that's okay. My alarm would have gone off shortly. . . . There was an accident last night and it was almost two before I got home. . . . Yep . . . What's up? . . . You did? When? . . . I was about to give up hope of ever hearing from Jackson again. What did they say? . . . She's not, huh? Are they sure? . . . I see. Well, I'm glad the other children are safe with relatives, but that doesn't help us with finding out who Amy is. . . . I know." A longer pause followed and then Justin said good bye and replaced the phone. Falling back onto his pillow, he flung an arm over his face and groaned. He didn't want to get up.

At last, shoving back the blankets, he swung his feet over the side of the bed and sat up. He would be expected at the hospital in a little over an hour. A quick shower woke him up fully and, sitting down, he picked up his Bible. He had been so dead with sleep when he got home that he hadn't read it before bed as he usually did.

After spending time on his knees, Justin prepared to walk over to the hospital. Stepping outside he sniffed the air. Spring. Soon the snow would be gone and everything would turn into a muddy mess until the grass turned green and the ground had a chance to dry.

"Morgan!"

Justin turned his head as he entered the hospital lobby. Dr. Wright was striding quickly towards him with a serious expression on his face. "What's up, Wright?"

"I just tried your place and you weren't there. I'm glad you came. We need to talk. Your office?"

Nodding, but puzzled, Justin led the way. "What's going on?" Dr. Morgan asked, seeing his fellow physician's sober face.

"We may be in for trouble," Dr. Wright began. "We've had eight patients brought in with the same symptoms. And they aren't even from the same areas. Morgan, if we get a few more with the same thing, I'd say we were in for an epidemic. And this spring weather isn't helping."

An epidemic. Justin recalled the one time in his residency when an epidemic had swept over the city. The hospital had run out of beds and it was weeks before he felt completely caught up on sleep.

Rebekah A. Morris

~23~

While he thought, Dr. Morgan had pulled on his white jacket. "Well, let's not wait for an epidemic. Let's say there is one and prepare for it now. What are the details. We'll need to make sure all the rooms are ready. Every nurse, or hospital worker should be alerted to stand by. Are there still extra cots over in the storage room of the hall? Good. We'll send someone over later to find out how many there are so we'll know how we stand in regard to beds."

He pulled out his chair and, grabbing a piece of paper, sat down and reached for his pen. "Okay, I want details, Wright. What are the symptoms and how old are the patients?"

One thing Dr. Justin Morgan enjoyed greatly was managing and planning for this little hospital. Many of the things, such as bed linens, towels, and dishes in the kitchen, he left for others to take care of, but when it came to arranging his hospital for a possible epidemic, Justin was in his element. All thoughts of Amy and Adam's phone call vanished. It was time to work and this was something he could do.

The epidemic did come, sweeping through the town

and up into the tiny hamlets nearby. Dr. Stern, called from
the hospital in Jackson, came out with a few assistants and
remained, lending a hand and offering advice. The spring-
like weather remained for two weeks and then a sudden
snowstorm blew down from the north and blanketed the
mountain in a fresh layer of cold snow. After that, the
epidemic seemed to lose strength, and in another week,
there were only a dozen patients left in the hospital
recovering.

Seated with Dr. Morgan in his office, Dr. Stern,
leaning back in his chair, said, "You and your staff did a
great job these last few weeks, Morgan."

"We couldn't have done it without all the prayers
going up and without your help, sir."

Dr. Stern smiled, "Without prayers, no, but my help
really wasn't needed. Any other doctor could have done as
much. That is one thing I was wanting to mention to you.
Have you ever considered adding a fifth doctor to your
staff? You seem to be busy enough to make use of one
more. It would also relieve the almost constant strain on
the four of you. With a fifth one, two of you could easily get
away for a day or two and not worry about being needed."

"I won't say it hasn't crossed my mind several times,"
Justin admitted. "At first I wasn't sure we'd actually need
one, but the longer we are open, the more we seem to be
needed. I know Philips wants to stay on here once he's
finished his internship, but that won't be for another year.
Do you know of anyone who would be willing to work here
for a year? There is a chance we might still want him
around even after Philips comes on, but I can't guarantee a
job."

"Actually, I do. Dr. Nye is a friend of mine from
Jackson. He was talking to me earlier this winter about

wanting to find a smaller hospital. He much prefers a quieter town and the possibility of knowing patients on a more personal level, such as you get up here."

For a few moments Dr. Morgan sat in thoughtful silence. At last he spoke. "I'll have to talk things over with the others, but if you recommend him, and he's interested, I'm willing to give him a try."

Dr. Stern stood up. "I'll have a talk with him then," he promised. "Let me know what you decide."

"I'll do that." Justin had risen also and now held out his hand. "Thank you again for coming out and helping, Dr. Stern. It was much appreciated!"

Gripping the offered hand, Dr. Stern flashed a tired smile. "Glad to do it. Now I've got to be heading back to Jackson. Has everyone else already gone?"

Justin nodded. "Yes, Harrel, Miller and Jacobson left yesterday. We'll be back to our usual staff after you leave. Thanks again."

With the epidemic in town, the Morgan family had remained up in their cabin, waiting to hear word from Justin that all was well. They had all enjoyed the spring-like weather. A considerable amount of snow had melted, and every time Danny was allowed to go outside, he managed to come in covered with mud but with a beaming face. Amy and Jenny also ventured outside but their interests centered on staying clean.

The sudden snowfall which helped end the epidemic in town was a source of tears for Danny, for he wasn't allowed to go out as much. Even Sara and Amy were dismal for a while.

But at last spring arrived as all springs do. The sun

shone for days on end, melting even the highest piles of snow and drying up the ground. The grass began to turn green, and here and there brave flowers poked up their heads and looked about as though making sure winter had really gone and taken its cold blanket with it. As the days lengthened, the warmth of the sun grew stronger and Adam plowed the garden.

To Amy, every day seemed to be filled with new surprises. She had taken to heart Adam's advice and was learning to trust her Lord with each new day. It wasn't always easy, as she would find herself startled or confused by some unexpected thing; her confidence was growing though.

With the arrival of the new doctor at the hospital, Justin found he was able to get away more often and spend time up at the cabin with his family. He was anxious to see how Amy was doing. He rejoiced to see her improvement. Not only was her health greatly improved by all the sunshine and fresh air, but her spirits had lifted. One thing still troubled him; who was she and where had she come from?

As soon as he had been able, Adam had set off on another trip of investigation, crossing the pass and visiting the towns and small villages but without success. No one had heard of or seen any of the trio and no one had a clue about where they might have come from. This news was a disappointment not only to the Morgan men, but Sara and Mrs. Morgan were equally troubled.

"She's got to have come from somewhere!" Sara almost groaned. The family were sitting in the office while Amy had the children outside walking in the sunshine.

"But where?" Mr. Morgan looked around the room. "I sent information about them to every city nearby, but nothing has turned up. Adam has personally checked all the towns and still nothing."

"Mother, what are you thinking?" Justin stopped his pacing and waited.

"Well, perhaps you should turn everything over to the F.B.I. Don't they try to find missing people?"

Mr. Morgan nodded slowly. "Yes, but Amy and the children aren't missing."

"But maybe they are missing, from somewhere else." Mrs. Morgan shrugged. "It was just a thought."

"There aren't any agents here, but—"

"I could drive over to Jackson," Adam offered.

Justin had resumed his pacing. After taking several turns across the room, he stopped. "But see here, so far, all the searching we've done has been quiet, so to speak. I don't want Amy to know we're doing all this. I'm afraid it will worry her and she'll start trying to remember again."

"But wouldn't that be good, if she did remember?" Sara asked.

"Perhaps. But fretting over it and trying to force herself to remember is only going to make things worse. When she remembers, if she remembers, I have a feeling it's going to be a shock."

"Why? You don't think it was just a blow to the head that brought about her condition?"

"That's probably what caused it, but I don't think it is a physical problem that is preventing her from remembering. From watching her and her reactions to different things, I have a feeling there is something very difficult, maybe even frightening, in her past that is being shut off by her subconscious." Frowning, he tried to explain it better. "It's like this. You have a room with a closet. Usually the closet is open and you can see what is inside. But one day something horrible happens, a rattlesnake gets in there."

Sara shuddered. One thing she hated was rattlesnakes.

"You slam the door and lock it, and in your horror, you throw the key someplace. And later, even when the fear has subsided, you can't open the door because you don't have the key. It's a poor illustration, I know. But I think Amy's mind is kind of like that. Something occurred in her past and then when whatever caused her injuries happened, it was like the door slamming shut and the key being tossed away. Someday I think she'll find the key and everything will come back. Maybe not all at once, but it could. But until that key is found, she's not going to remember, and the harder she tries to force the door open, the tighter it is going to stick." He paused and looked at his brother. "If you do go to the F.B.I. see if you can get them to search without bothering Amy."

Adam nodded. There was no time for more conversation as Danny's voice was heard and the trio was seen approaching.

Sara went outside to join Amy, and Mrs. Morgan departed to start lunch. Looking out the window Mr. Morgan sighed. "The poor girl. She's been through so much. And if what you say is true, Justin—if her past is troubling, how much harder will it be when it does come back. Not only did she have to live through it, but then to suddenly have it all come back again." He shook his head. Amy had grown to be like another daughter to Mr. Morgan and he hated the thought of her hurt again.

"She does have the Lord with her this time," Adam remarked quietly.

Justin nodded. "Yes. And she has everyone here. I just pray it won't be too much for her when it does come."

Mr. Morgan looked at his son. "You think it was something that troubling?"

"Yes," Justin replied simply. "I can't explain it, but—" He shook his head.

* * *

It was a glorious spring day. The air was warm and the mountainside fairly gleamed with color. Flowers of every hue carpeted the slope and everywhere birds sang and chirped. Up above, the sky was a deep blue, the kind that lets you look up and up and still feel as though there is no end to the blue dome. Not a cloud was to be seen in any direction, and the sun, that brilliant ball of flaming light, beckoned so appealingly that it was difficult to remain indoors for even a few moments.

Inside the Morgan cabin all was hustle and bustle. The windows and doors had all been opened, and with this enticement, it was almost impossible to get things ready. Mrs. Morgan and Heather hurried about the kitchen packing food while Sara tried to help, but every few minutes she would run outside. Amy had her hands full trying to keep the little ones from getting under foot or running outdoors by themselves. And the men were busy collecting supplies. The family was going on a hike. They were even going to eat lunch outside! Erin Louise had told this bit of news to Amy in an excited whisper. She would have told her more, but Amy had caught sight of Danny and Lucas escaping through the open door and had run after them. Captain, too polite and well trained to enter the house though the door was open, barked at the doorway as though urging those within to hurry.

At last everything was ready. Mr. Morgan and his sons and son-in-law hoisted the packs onto their backs, the ladies corralled the children, and they set off; Captain frolicked around like a puppy in his delight. Amy said not a word as they began to climb the mountain behind the cabin. A well worn path led them up and around until they paused where a bench had been built and turned to look down into the valley. The cabin looked like a doll's house and the towering trees near it seemed shrunken in size. Someone pointed out the town in the distance. Amy was speechless. It was all so lovely, and it would have been quiet had the children not been there.

"I could just stay here all day," Amy thought, her eyes slowly drifting over the scene below and then rising to the mountain peaks beyond where a lone eagle soared on a current of air.

"Amy." Someone touched her arm.

She looked up. Nearly everyone had started off again and only Justin, with Jenny on his shoulders, had remained. "Oh, I'm sorry." She turned quickly. "I was just admiring the view."

"It is something to see, isn't it?" Justin agreed, glancing down once more. "When I was at home more, this was my favorite place to come and think, or read or pray. Many a morning I'd bring my Bible up here just as the sun was rising. Somehow I always felt closer to God up here."

"I can see why." And Amy looked back at the spot they had just left.

The climb grew a little steeper and the children had to be helped along, Lucas and Danny catching rides on shoulders when their little legs gave out, while Jenny kept her seat on Justin's shoulders where she patted his head and chattered in her own baby language which was difficult to understand.

A resting place was reached with sighs of relief from several of the members, but after a short break, they were ready to set off again.

Amy wondered where they would end up, but was content to follow the leading of the others, until they came to the woods. Here she hesitated. Something made her cringe inwardly about entering the shady trees, though the sun had grown quite warm.

"It can't be that bad," she assured herself. "Everyone else is going in. Perhaps it is just a little bit of woods." Resolutely she started forward, but the farther into the trees she went, the faster her heart began to beat. Every sound seemed twice as loud and she wiped her clammy hands on her clothes. Her feet slowed down and she glanced around. It didn't look frightening, but she couldn't escape the feeling she had. Should she say something? But what would they think of her?

~24~

"Is everything all right, Amy?" Justin's quiet voice spoke behind her.

"No. I want to get out of these trees!" Her voice was a higher pitch than normal.

"There isn't much farther to go," he said.

Amy shook her head. "I don't think I can do it. I . . . I . . . Justin, I'm scared!" There she had admitted it.

"All right, we'll go the other way." He called ahead to his mother to let her know their change of path, and then turned. "Come on, we'll get back into the sunlight."

Amy wanted to run, but Justin wisely set a steady pace. He knew her nameless fears, he read them in her eyes, but running would only make things worse. To help keep her mind off of her feelings, he started to whistle.

At last they reached the edge of the woods and stepped out into the sunlight. Amy drew a long quivering breath and a shudder raced through her frame. "Thank you," she whispered.

Justin gave her a minute to collect herself and then, setting Jenny down, he said, "Come along, gals, we've got a harder climb this way."

"Oh, why don't I just go back to the house and you

and Jenny can go on and catch up with the others." Amy looked down the sunny path they had come up. "I don't mind, honestly I don't."

But Justin wouldn't hear of it. "No way, this is a family picnic, and you are part of the family and are coming too. Now let's go."

"But—"

"No buts, Amy." Justin's voice was firm and he started off slowly, holding Jenny's hand in his. There was no path, but Justin followed the outskirts of the woods and seemed to know where he was going. Every few steps he had to pause to let Jenny pick another flower. There were no stems on them, but she didn't care and clutched them tightly in her hot, little hand.

Hesitating, Amy remained where she stood on the path. She wanted to enjoy the picnic, but she was afraid. What other nameless fears lurked on the trail ahead? It might be better if she returned to the house. But she wasn't sure Justin would let her. Why couldn't he understand? "Justin!"

He neither turned nor answered, but continued a few steps farther, talking to Jenny.

"Justin, I want to go home."

Still no reply came.

She was tempted to start for home right then but was afraid the family might worry about her if no one knew she had gone. She would just run up and tell Justin first. He wouldn't stop her if he really knew how hard it was for her. "If only my leg would start to hurt," she thought, "then I'd have a real excuse and not just this 'something' which haunts me." Timidly she stepped off the path and hurried after the pair up ahead.

"Justin," she called again as she neared them.

This time he turned with a smile. "Aren't the flowers beautiful? Heather and I used to come up here every spring and summer and pick bouquets for Mother every week. I'm not sure if I like the spring flowers or the later summer ones better." He looked fondly down at the little figure eagerly filling her chubby hands with color. "Come on, Jenny, we've got a mountain to climb; then you can show your treasures to Grandma." He held out his hands and Jenny trotted over to be picked up and set upon his broad shoulders once more.

"I came to tell you," Amy began, finding it hard to express herself, "that I . . . I'm going to go back to the house. I . . . I just can't go on."

For a moment Justin said not a word but only looked at her. She felt her cheeks grow hot and dropped her eyes. "I don't need anyone to go with me. I . . . I can go alone."

"Amy," Justin said at last, reaching out and lifting her chin with his finger. "Are you trying to run away from your fears?"

"Yes." The word was the faintest of whispers, and she kept her eyes off his face.

"That's not very trusting, is it?"

"Wha . . . what do you mean?"

He hooked his thumbs on the straps of his pack. "Are you forgetting Who said He will never leave you? You are trying to face these fears on your own. You can't do that."

The eyes that lifted and met his suddenly filled with tears. "I was forgetting. But I can't seem to remember when I just suddenly feel— Oh, you don't know what it's like to feel the fear and terror that grip me!"

"True, I don't know. But Jesus does." Quietly Justin turned and started walking onward again. "And it is He who said 'it is I, be not afraid.' Amy, life isn't always easy, even for those of us who can remember. Troubling times come to each of us. That's just a part of life. It's how we respond to those times that either makes us stronger, or a weaker prey for the next trouble or fear."

Walking beside him, Amy forgot about going home. "But it's so hard! I told myself it was all right, back there, but I could no more get away from the frightening 'something' than . . . than I could fly!"

"You aren't expected to escape alone, Amy. You do have a Refuge and a Fortress and a Shield. You know, those things aren't going to be of much use if there are no troubles or temptations or fears, are they?"

The reply was slow. "No, I guess not." Then her tone changed. "But why did I feel that way about the woods?" she demanded. "I wanted to scream!" She glared at the innocent trees reaching out sheltering branches and sighing in the gentle breeze.

Justin couldn't keep back a smile at the fierceness in the voice which only moments before had been more pitiful than a kitten. "Amy, before you and the children arrived at our cabin, you had been wandering in the mountains for probably several days. During that time there is no doubt that you would have been in the woods quite a bit. Now, don't you think it's possible that when you were in the woods today, your mind was replaying some of the fears you felt when you were lost?"

Amy didn't answer.

The woods on their left ended and Justin lifted Jenny from his shoulders. "Here we have some climbing to do," he told the little girl, "and I don't want you falling off your horse." He turned to Amy. "Do you see that lone tree up there?" And he pointed. When she nodded he went on.

"That's where we're headed. I'll go first to give you a hand if you need it. You'll probably have to use your hands and feet to reach the top, but you can do it. Do you want a drink first?"

"Yes, please."

After a refreshing drink of the cool water from Justin's canteen, they started climbing. Several times Amy thought she wouldn't be able to make it, but each time, Justin would give her a helping hand and some encouragement.

At last that lone tree was reached and Amy collapsed on the ground to catch her breath. She had forgotten her fears in the rough climb, and now her cheeks glowed and her eyes sparkled. "Oh, what a view!" she exclaimed when she could speak again without panting.

"Isn't it something?" And Justin leaned against the tree.

"I feel like I'm on top of the world."

"He maketh my feet like hinds' feet and setteth me upon my high places," quoted Justin quietly. "We'd better be going. We still have a little ways left to go. But it isn't as hard as this last part."

When at last they reached the picnic grounds, they found the others just arriving.

"Did you come the other way?" Heather asked.

Amy nodded, sinking down with a sigh of relief. She was tired and her legs protested the very thought of moving.

Jenny, having been refreshed by a short nap in Justin's arms, was eager to show her poor wilted and crumpled flowers to Grandma and jabbered on about something while lunch was being set out.

Everyone ate with hearty appetites and then, as the adults stretched out to relax, the children were eager to play and raced about the mountain slope, chasing each other and having a delightful time. Not one of the adults was inclined to join them. Even Sara was content to remain where she was and watch. There wasn't much talk around the picnic blankets. The sun was warm, but the breeze kept it from growing uncomfortably so.

Sara broke the silence. "Whenever I come up here, I feel like there should be goats or cows that I must watch and that I should not be speaking English, but another language."

"Feeling a bit like Heidi?" Mrs. Morgan asked with a smile.

Sara laughed, "Until I think about walking all the way back home again. Then I wish I was a pioneer and had a horse to ride."

"Lazy," Justin teased.

"Yep," Sara admitted readily and grinned.

After a few more minutes, Mr. Morgan glanced down at his watch. "We'd better pack up and start heading back. We don't want to get home too late."

"Or we'll be too tired for church tomorrow," added Mrs. Morgan, beginning to gather empty dishes.

"Well, one thing's for sure," Timothy remarked, assisting his wife in folding up one of the blankets. "We'll have lighter packs going down."

"Ah, but no doubt you'll have to carry some tired child." Justin grinned at his brother-in-law as he gave an exaggerated groan.

With everyone helping it didn't take long to pack things up. Sara's whistle had brought both the children and

Captain running, and the family was ready to set off for home.

Amy expected Justin to start back the way they had come, but he didn't seem to remember they had come a different way. He followed the others down the gently sloping mountainside with apparently no thought for her.

"I can't go that way," Amy thought. "Doesn't he know that? I can't go through the woods! I tried." Could she go back alone the way they had come up? Timidly she turned and looked up the hill. Should she try it?

"Amy?" Heather's voice startled her and she turned around quickly. "Sorry, I didn't mean to scare you. Aren't you ready to go yet?"

"Can we go back the way Justin and I came?"

Heather shook her head. "No. Coming up is one thing, but going down—let's just say it's a lot harder going down. That's how Justin broke his arm when he was ten. Come on, we'll have to hurry to catch up with the others."

But Amy hung back. "I . . . I can't go that way."

"Yes, you can," Heather assured. "Remember, 'I can do all things through Christ which strengtheneth me'."

"But I panic in the woods!" Amy was almost in tears. Would no one understand her fright?

Heather was not to be swayed by tears. "Did you keep your mind on what is true and right and lovely? I thought not. And you didn't have anyone there to talk with."

"Justin was there," Amy whimpered. "But I can't do it, Heather, I can't!"

~25~

Heather put an arm around the girl's waist and drew her forward. "We'll cross one bridge at a time when we come to it. You know, when a cowboy falls off his horse or is thrown off, he gets up, dusts himself off and climbs back on. If he doesn't, sometimes a feeling of fear takes over and he doesn't want to ever get back on. You have been frightened of the woods sometime, but you haven't gone back into them on a bright sunny day and conquered that fear. Until you do, you'll always be afraid of them."

"But—"

Heather laughed. "Buts don't work at my house, Amy. Come on, it looks like Justin is waiting for us." Seizing her hand, Heather started at a rapid pace, almost pulling the reluctant Amy along with her.

When the girls reached Justin, they noticed the others had gone on ahead. "Ready to go?" he asked, rising from the large rock he had been sitting on.

"Yes," Heather smiled, but Amy shook her head.

No one noticed.

Amy wanted to ask Justin if they couldn't go back the other way, but she hesitated. He was talking to his sister as they strolled along. There weren't any woods in sight. A sudden and happy thought struck Amy. Perhaps there was another way to get home that Justin hadn't mentioned. Surely he wouldn't force her to walk through the woods if she was terrified of them. Thus assured by her own thoughts, Amy joined in the conversation and the tense feeling of fear vanished.

Amy was in the middle of a story of something Danny had done only a few days before when she suddenly realized they had already entered the woods. Her story stopped short and she froze, looking about. Everything was quiet and still. She shivered. A tingling, like the feet of a small mouse, ran up her back, down her arms and then raced back down her back and into her legs. She was going to scream!

"Amy!" Justin's sharp voice made her turn her head to look at him. "Stop imagining. You cannot face life afraid of every shadow. There is nothing here that is going to hurt you."

"Just look how pretty the light is shining down through the leaves up ahead," Heather pointed out. "Later in the summer the leaves will have grown, but now they let in so much sunlight."

Cautiously Amy followed Heather a few steps farther down the trail. She had to admit that the filtered light was pretty, but something in the back of her brain kept tormenting her with dark and frightening thoughts. Something Justin had said earlier came back. "Perhaps that is the reason."

"What is?" Justin asked, and Amy realized that she had spoken her thoughts aloud.

"Maybe being lost with the children made me afraid of the woods. I don't really remember much about that time except there seemed to be trees everywhere and we couldn't get out. It was dark and the sun wasn't shining. The children cried. There was pain and . . . and . . . Oh, I can't think about it!" Her words ended in a low cry and she stopped to bury her face in her hands.

Instantly Heather had her arms around the girl and hugged her close. There were tears in her own eyes. "But that's over now, Amy. You were led out of the woods and to help. Jesus Christ is right beside you. You won't be alone ever again. Now you can face the future with your hand in His."

No one said a word for some time. Amy remained in Heather's arms with her face hidden. In the silence the sound of a few birds singing in the trees and the whisper of the wind could be heard. A scratching sound was heard and Amy flinched.

"Amy," Heather whispered, "look up slowly. It's a squirrel come to see us."

Timidly, like a frightened doe, Amy lifted her head. A squirrel had paused part way down the trunk of a nearby tree and was regarding them. Seeing they made no move, he flipped his tail and chattered before turning and scampering up to the safety of a higher limb where he continued his scolding.

Justin chuckled. "I think he's trying to tell us to go away; and I agree. We ought to be moving along."

Somehow, after her cry, the woods didn't seem as frightening to Amy, though she breathed a sigh of relief when they were finally out on the other side.

"You did it, Amy," Heather praised. "I knew you could."

"Not without you and Justin, and," she added softly, "my Shepherd."

"Do you think you can face life with Him, now?" Justin asked.

Amy nodded. It would be hard work at times, for the fears which came were sudden and sometimes overwhelmingly strong, but after seeing her fear of the woods conquered, she knew with Christ, she could face anything.

"I think she's made great progress towards a full recovery," Justin remarked to his dad and Adam later that evening after the others had retired. The men had taken a stroll in the moonlight and had reached the road in silence before Justin spoke.

"Do you think she'll remember?" Mr. Morgan asked.

"It's hard to tell. She might. From things she has said about having glimpses of scenes or sounds come into her mind, like the church bells, I think her mind is trying to remember, but I think there is still something which happened shortly before she and the children were lost in the mountains that is keeping it closed. What that thing is, I have no idea."

"We'll keep praying," Adam assured softly.

"That's all any of us can do right now. Pray and be there for her if and when the memories come back or she is facing an unknown fear."

* * *

It was a cloudy, dreary day. In town Dr. Morgan had just finished his shift at the hospital and was strolling toward his rooms. Gazing up at the mountain peaks shrouded in a fine mist, he shook his head. A steady rain would be more pleasant than the weather they were having.

"Good afternoon, Doctor."

Justin stopped and turned his head. "Oh, good afternoon, John. How's that little son of yours doing?"

John Duffey grinned. "He's just wonderful, Doctor. My wife couldn't be more proud of our little fellow. He's the best baby I've ever seen and so good natured. Why, Doctor, if you'll believe it, he's got my mother so wrapped around his little finger that you'd never know her." He chuckled. "I can't thank you enough, Doctor, for making me take my wife to see Dr. Hollend."

Justin laughed. "No need to thank me. You would have had the baby whether or not you had seen Dr. Hollend. I'm just afraid I would have been called instead of him when he arrived."

John laughed too. "That's true; Mother would have sent for you right off, if we hadn't known. But Doctor, I've got a rather strange question to ask you."

"All right, shoot." Justin shoved one hand into his pocket and leaned against a light post.

There was a moment of hesitation before John said, "That girl your family took in."

"Amy?"

"Yeah, I think that's what Clara said her name was. Did you ever find out where she came from or who she is?"

Justin shook his head. "No, we've tried everything we can think of, but nothing has turned up."

"Hmm, you know I do a lot of traveling, and, well, last time I was out, I was eating at a restaurant in Newell and I overheard some men talking. They were pilots and mentioned refueling in Jackson. They also mentioned something about a plane crash. Well, I got curious 'cause I didn't remember anything about any plane crash and so I asked them. They said someone had spotted what looked to be a wrecked plane in the mountains and these men had flown over the wreck to check it out. Said it looked like it had been there a while, at least before winter set in. They asked me if I knew anything about it, but I didn't." He paused and scratched his face. "But that got me curious, so I asked a few more questions and found out that a group had gone out on foot to see if they could discover what plane it was. The pilots said it looked rather burned. These men didn't know what had been discovered by the ground party, but suggested I check with the airport or police in Jackson. I forgot about it all until I saw you folks in church yesterday. I was wanting to ask you or Adam about it then, but didn't get the chance."

"Did you ever check with the airport?"

John Duffey shook his head. "No, I never got around to it. My little fellow is a mighty strong magnet to keeping me home." He grinned happily. "But it was only last Thursday I met those fellows. Do you think it might mean anything?"

"It's hard to say. So far every lead has turned into a dead end."

"They have to have come from someplace, and someone somewhere has got to know something about them."

"And *sometime* we might find *something* out," Justin chuckled. A large drop of water hit his head and he glanced up. "Looks like that mist might be getting ready to turn into real rain soon."

"Sure does. I'll not keep you any longer, Doctor. Hope you can find something out."

"Me too, John." The two men shook hands. "I'll let

you know if we do. Thanks."

By the time Justin had reached his rooms and taken off his rain jacket, the drops were falling pretty steadily. "If it weren't raining, I'd go down and see if Dad's still at his office in town. Oh, well, a phone call will do just fine."

Mr. Morgan was in and Justin related the conversation to him, ending with, "What do you think, Dad, could they have come from a crashed airplane?"

"Justin, anything is possible. But we've tried so many things, don't get your hopes up. You don't know where this plane was located?"

"No. Just that it was in these mountains and the search pilots refueled in Jackson."

"Not much to go off of, but I'll make a few phone calls and see if I can find out anything. I'll let you know. But it could be days, if they haven't figured out what plane it is, so don't get impatient."

"I know. Thanks, Dad."

After he hung up, Justin slowly paced his rooms. This was the hardest part of all this mystery—waiting and not knowing. At last he dropped to his knees and took the whole trouble to the feet of his Savior.

There wasn't much going on in the Morgan cabin. With the steady rain falling outside, there was no chance to work in the garden. Amy had discovered a delight in the planting of tiny seedlings and digging in the dirt. But today had to be spent inside. Danny had gone into town with Mr. Morgan and Adam, and Jenny was somewhere with Sara. There was an aimlessness to Amy's wanderings through the house and she wondered how she should pass the time. She had grown tired of reading and wanted something different. She didn't know why, but the last few days she had felt restless. Seeing some music books lying on the piano, she stopped and picked one up. Flipping a few pages she came across a song she didn't remember ever hearing Sara play. Silently she sat down and, without thinking, placed her hands gently on the piano keys.

"That's a lovely song, Sara," Mrs. Morgan remarked entering the living room a little while later. "What is it called?"

A blonde head lifted from behind the piano and Amy gasped, "Mother, I can play. I was playing it! I don't know how to play the piano, but I did."

'What's going on?" Sara asked, hurrying in. "Is Justin here? Amy!"

Amy was staring at the black and white keys before her. "I played it," she whispered. "I played a song."

"Can you play another one?" Mrs. Morgan asked as she and Sara hurried across the room.

"I—I don't know. I didn't mean to play this one. I just sat down to read the words and the next thing I knew, I was playing it."

"Try another one," Sara suggested. "If you really can play the piano, we can play together sometimes."

Turning a few pages, Amy found another song that caught her fancy, and timidly she began to play. The notes floated around her like bright winged butterflies. She didn't know how she knew which notes on the page belonged to which keys, but somehow she did. When the song ended, she looked up, her face glowing, eyes sparkling with a light never seen in them before.

"I can play!" Pressing her hands over her flushed cheeks, Amy drew in several quick excited breaths. "I—"
Tears began to trickle down her cheeks.

Alarmed, Sara asked, "Amy, what's wrong?"

But Amy shook her head. "Oh, Sara, I can play songs!" was all she could say, smiling through the tears as she stroked the black and white keys tenderly.

Mrs. Morgan bent and kiss the flushed face and whispered, "Play all you want to, Amy, Dear."

And Amy did. Almost the entire afternoon was spent at the instrument, drawing out first one song and then another. She couldn't play like Sara could, but she could follow the notes which were written and found great satisfaction in playing some of her favorite hymns.

When Mr. Morgan and Adam returned from town with Danny, they found the new musician still at the piano. Adam didn't say anything, but Mr. Morgan came over and remarked, "So, now I have three musically inclined children."

Amy looked up with a bright smile which seemed to Mr. Morgan to light up the room. "Oh, Dad, I can play!" Those seemed to be the only words Amy could find to express her delight over her newly recovered ability.

That night Amy lay awake a long time thinking. She had loved the sound of the piano ever since she had come to stay at the Morgan home, and now she wondered why it had taken her so long to discover she could play. "Perhaps I was scared," she thought. "No, I don't think I was scared, I just didn't know I could. . . . I wonder what made me start playing today? I didn't have any intention of playing. I wonder if I know more about music than I think I do." She turned restlessly in her bed. "I wish it were morning so I could play again. But I must get to sleep."

She turned over again and closed her eyes. But it was

no use. The excitement of discovering she could play would not let her sleep. For over an hour she tossed and turned, trying to order her brain to cease whirling. She counted backwards from one hundred, she tried thinking about the book she had read the day before, but nothing worked.

Finally she gave up. "Well, if I can't sleep, I might as well do something."

Throwing back her blankets, Amy sat up and reached for her warm robe. Though the days were pleasant, the nights were still chilly.

~26~

Moments later, Amy tiptoed down the hall and into the dark living room. There was no glow from the fireplace and the only sounds were the steady ticking of the clock and the gentle patter of raindrops against the windows.

Sliding onto the bench before the baby grand piano, Amy's hand reached up and snapped on a small light. She could at least read the words to the hymns, she decided. The song book was open to the evening hymns.

Upstairs, Mr. Morgan stepped out into the hall. The soft sound of a piano drifted up from the living room. Quietly, he started down the hall.

Across the hall, Sara opened her door and put out a sleepy face. "Dad," she whispered, "what is she doing? Doesn't she know it's the middle of the night?"

"Somehow, Sara, I doubt if she cares right now," Mr. Morgan replied in hushed tones. "Go back to bed. I'll make sure she's all right."

Sara's head withdrew and her door shut.

Continuing down the hall, his stocking feet making no noise on the carpet, Mr. Morgan couldn't help but wonder if Amy was awake or playing in her sleep. When he reached the head of the walkway, he paused and leaned on the railing watching. Amy wasn't asleep, he decided, and she didn't look ill as his wife had feared. "She's just making up for all the months she didn't know she could play," he finally decided before he straightened. Since no one else seemed disturbed, he didn't have the heart to put an end to Amy's playing. "She'll go to bed when she's ready."

For the next two days, all Amy wanted to do was play the piano. Only when Danny begged for a story was Amy willing to leave the world of music so long shut to her. At meal times she quit playing reluctantly and then hurried back to the piano as soon as the dishes were done.

On the third day the sun rose in a cloudless sky and the air was alive with the songs of birds. Tiny insects buzzed and hopped about and Captain barked at everything in his delight over the sunny day. Turning into the Morgan driveway, Justin could see his mother, Danny and Jenny in the garden. He stopped the truck and got out, rubbing Captain's ears when he came to greet him. "Yes, boy, it's good to see you too. But I didn't come to play."

As Justin hurried up onto the porch, he heard the sounds of the piano. "Sara must be in a musical mood," he thought with a smile, opening the door.

"Hi, Justin," his sister greeted him as he stepped inside. "Are you here for Adam? What are you staring at?"

"Who is playing the piano?" he demanded, blinking at his sister.

"Amy."

"Amy? What?" In a few steps, Justin was in the doorway. The light head never looked up and Justin backed away. "What is going on?"

Sara couldn't help a slight chuckle at his expression. Rapidly she filled him in on Amy's discovery. "And she's been playing it almost constantly since. Why, Justin, that first night she got up and started playing the piano in the middle of the night! I don't know when she went to bed. Only Danny asking for a story will get her away from that thing if it isn't time to eat."

"Well!" Justin couldn't think of anything else to say.

Adam came down the stairs and into the hall. "Ready to go?" he asked.

"Huh?" Justin blinked. "Oh, yeah. Sara, see if you can't get Amy outside a little while today."

"I'll try, but don't count on anything." Sara followed her brothers onto the porch and waved when they drove away.

There was silence in the truck for several miles and then Justin spoke. "Adam, do you think Amy has remembered anything since she started playing the piano?"

Adam shook his head. "I don't know. She hasn't said anything, but I haven't asked her either."

Another long silence followed before Justin spoke again. "I wonder if this trip will be worthwhile."

The police in Jackson had called Mr. Morgan and said that they might have some information. Justin, finding that with Dr. Nye now on staff he could be spared for the day, offered to go with Adam. He didn't want to remain at home and spend his day wondering what Adam was finding out. Surely soon they would discover something about Amy's past. They just had to. She couldn't have just appeared from nowhere.

"It's been months since I've been to Jackson," Justin remarked, turning off the highway. "I've forgotten how busy a city like this is."

"I couldn't stand to live here," Adam agreed, pointing

out the turn Justin needed to take. "Too rushed."

"Just think how big a city like Newell is. This will seem small then."

"It's still too crowded."

Justin had to agree. He much preferred the small mountain town he had grown up in to the large, bustling metropolis of Jackson, even if by comparison Jackson was a small city.

Pulling into the parking lot near the police station, the Morgan brothers got out and headed toward the door. Whatever the police had discovered could either change Amy's life or start the searching all over again.

The officer at the desk looked up as they entered. "Yes? Can I help you?"

"I'm Adam Morgan and this is my brother, Justin. We were called and told that Chief Taylor wanted to talk with us today."

Pressing a button, the officer spoke, "Adam Morgan and his brother are here, sir."

A deep voice answered, "Send them on back."

"Yes, sir." The officer stood up and opened a door. "Just go down the hall to the second door on your right. The chief is waiting for you."

After thanking the officer, Adam and Justin stepped through the doorway. Adam knew where he was going, having been there before, and Justin was content to follow.

Three men were sitting in conference when Adam and Justin paused before the open door. The chief of police looked up and waved them in. "Come in, both of you. Adam," he remarked, rising slightly and holding out his hand, "it's good to see you again."

"And you, sir. Chief, I'd like you to meet my older

brother, Justin."

Justin shook hands with the chief as that man asked, "Are you the doctor who handled the case of Amy and the two children?"

"Yes, I am."

The chief nodded. "Do sit down, both of you. Oh, let me introduce Rick McDonald. He's with the F.B.I." A man with light hair and keen blue eyes, rose and shook hands. "And this is Gil Conway. He's with the forest rangers and was the head of the party that visited the downed plane." The other man, a rugged, yet friendly man, whose dark hair fell over a high forehead, flashed a brief smile and nodded. Chief Taylor leaned back in his chair. "There, now that introductions are over, Rick, suppose you take over. After all, that plane crashed outside of city limits."

The F.B.I. agent nodded. "Sure thing, Chief. I'll start right off by saying we still don't know if the girl and the children did come from this plane. We're still checking on some things. But we thought it would be a good idea to try and piece together what information we do have. Doctor," he turned to Justin, "I'm glad you came along, as we may need your help."

"I'll do what I can," Justin promised.

Rick nodded. "Headquarters in Washington has been notified about the three, but so far no word has come back matching them with any missing person. Now, Conway, suppose you tell us about what you found."

The forest ranger nodded and flipped open his small notebook. "When we reached the plane, it was obvious that there had been a fire. It hadn't blown up because of a lack of fuel. At this point we aren't sure if the plane went down because of that fact or if there was another reason. Both wings were torn nearly off the body of the plane. There were no bodies inside and no signs of the remains of any outside. Since this plane wasn't found soon after the wreck, any traces of where the pilot, co-pilot and any passengers may have gone were completely wiped away. What we did discover, however, is the identification numbers on the plane." He paused and glanced over at the F.B.I. agent. "Rick, do you want to tell about that part now?"

"No, go ahead with everything else you discovered."

The ranger continued. "The inside was burned pretty bad, but we did find evidence of what we think were items from passengers. One was a baby shoe."

"How big?" Justin broke in to ask.

The ranger passed a piece of paper over to him. "We took a photo of it before turning it over to the F.B.I. for analyzation. Tell you anything?"

For a brief moment, Justin looked at the small, blackened shoe in the photograph. "Could any color be seen on it?"

"Besides black, no. But that's not saying there might not be color under the soot and smoke. We also found a necklace half buried in the ground under the tail of the plane." Another picture was handed to Justin and Adam who examined it closely.

"Was this sent to the lab also?" Adam asked, looking up.

"Yes. Anything we could salvage, which wasn't much, was sent there. Those are the only two items that make me think there were passengers on board." The ranger took the photos and slipped them back into his notebook before continuing. "Like I said before, there was no trace or trail of anyone. But I knew an old hermit lived a couple miles from the crash site and we headed there. This man is not what you might call inquisitive, so I wasn't sure if we'd discover anything. Turns out we did. He told us two men staggered to his cabin one night in the middle of a storm. One died only hours after arriving and the other must have had pneumonia, for he died before a week was out."

"Pilot and co-pilot?" Adam ventured to guess.

Heads nodded. "That's what we guessed right away," Conway said. "The hermit buried both men but kept what few things he found on them, just in case someone came looking for them. We got the name of one of the men from some papers found in his wallet." The ranger shut his notebook. "I think that about covers my info. Rick?"

The F.B.I. agent nodded. "We've checked the plane's identification numbers and found it to be a private plane belonging to one Logan Bridges out of Santa Rosa, California. He was the unidentified man who had been buried. He filed a flight plan with the airport to fly to Big Falls, Minnesota. He never arrived. As you can see by this map," he spread a map on the police chief's desk and pointed, "the direct flight would not have taken him anywhere near Jackson, Newell or anywhere even close."

"How'd he get so far off track?"

"Hard to say right now. We've got men checking what they can of the plane, to see if something went wrong. Here's another thing. According to when the flight was filed and how long it would have taken to reach this area," Rick pointed to the crash site, "it would have gone down during that big storm in the fall."

Justin's mind was collecting pieces of information almost faster than he could keep up. The storm, a plane crash, Amy's fright of the wind, fire and woods. Could it be that she and the children had been passengers in that plane? If so, why were they in the plane? Could they have become lost in the woods, separated from the pilot and co-pilot? "She never would have survived had she been with them. Or Jenny either." He spoke his thoughts aloud.

"What was that?" The F.B.I. agent turned at the sound of his words.

Justin looked up. "Sorry, I guess I was thinking aloud. Is there any way to find out for sure if Amy and the children were on that plane, or if they have relatives or family?"

"We have agents checking in Santa Rosa for family, friends, possible passengers for this flight or for neighbors who might know anything about the pilot or the co-pilot. Other agents are checking in Big Falls. I'm guessing it will be harder in Big Falls though."

"Why is that?" Adam asked.

"Because it doesn't appear that Bridges ever lived outside of California. We have sent pictures of the children and Amy on to both places, but it may take days, or longer, before we learn anything definite."

~27~

"It seems, sir," Adam remarked slowly, "that things fit together for Amy and the children to have been on that plane, but they also seemed to fit with the couple in the avalanche." He shook his head. "Could there have been other passengers, or family even, on the plane?"

Agent McDonald gave a slight smile. "Checking every angle, I like that. Neither the pilot or co-pilot were married that we know of. Could it have been other family members of Amy and the children? Possibly. At this point there is no way to tell just how many passengers there were."

Ranger Conway spoke up. "The plane was large enough for more than just three, but it was too burned out to know how many there were, since all the luggage was pretty much destroyed. We'll hopefully know more later."

Adam nodded.

"Any other ideas or questions?" Rick looked around the room.

All were silent, and several minutes ticked by as Adam and Justin thought. Then Justin spoke.

"From what I've heard just now, I'm inclined to think that Amy and the children did come from that airplane crash. That could explain why she has been frightened of fire at times. It would also explain what it was she had to get the children out of that was so frightening. The sound of the wind could have caused her panic because it brought back the sounds of the plane before it crashed. But even if they did come from the plane, who are they and where did they come from?"

"If we knew for sure which last name to give Amy, we might make headway on that," McDonald said slowly. "It could also be that her parents were on the plane when it crashed and they died in the mountains. If we could verify for sure how many passengers were on the plane, it would help. Another way to possibly find out who Amy is would be through someone who knew the pilot. Maybe he mentioned this flight to a friend or neighbor. But it has been several months, so any trail is going to be cold; but we'll keep searching."

There was more talking, analyzing, and speculations. Rick McDonald questioned Justin about the state the children and Amy were in when they arrived at the cabin. Did he think Amy's memory would return? Had either of the children given an hints as to where they had lived before? He wanted to know anything and everything about them which might help in the investigation. Finally he leaned back. "I can't think of a single thing more to ask you," he said.

Justin laughed. "Good. I don't think I could think of another answer."

The agent rose. "Thank you for coming out. I'm going to take this information to my office and get to work. Chief, thank you for the use of your office. And Conway, your information was invaluable." He shook hands with each one. "I'll keep you all informed. And Justin, Adam, if Amy should suddenly remember, let us know."

"We'll be sure to do that, sir," Justin replied, shaking the offered hand. "And, believe me, we want to know the answers to the whos, whats, when's, and hows as much as, or more than, the rest of you do."

"I imagine you do."

The drive home was quiet. Each brother was trying to process all the information they had received. It wasn't until they pulled off the highway that Justin spoke, "Why would she have been flying to Big Falls, Minnesota?"

Adam gave a snort. "Why would she be flying from Santa Rosa, California?"

"She lived there?"

"Maybe she lived in Minnesota."

Justin gave a sigh. "This is too much for my brain to handle. I think I'll try to think of something else for the rest of the day."

"Good luck," Adam said dryly.

No matter how hard Justin tried, after leaving Adam at Mr. Morgan's office where he would catch a ride home with their father, he couldn't get Amy, the plane crash and all the other details from his mind. Even while trying to read a new book, he saw on the pages the photos of the baby shoe and the necklace, instead of the words.

* * *

Another bright, sunny day had arrived on the mountain, and Amy felt like dancing as she left her room that morning. All night the window had been open and she had awakened to the songs of the birds and the scent of wildflowers blooming outside. Her heart was full of the joy and wonder of spring. A tune echoed in her head and bubbled forth in a low but happy song from her lips.

"Joyful, joyful we adore Thee,
God of glory, Lord of love.
Hearts unfold like flowers before Thee,
Opening to the Son above."

She wanted to go outside. For days she had been seated at the piano playing song after song, but today— today she knew she could leave the piano. The fear of forgetting how to play again was gone and her fingers longed to get dirty in the garden.

"Good morning, Amy," Mrs. Morgan smiled from a seat at the dining room table. "You look bright and sunny this morning."

"Good morning, Mother! I feel bright and sunny." She drew a deep breath of the fresh morning breeze. "Doesn't this air make you want to get outside and do something?"

Mrs. Morgan laughed. "Yes, it does. And I'm sure I will be outside, but it will be down at Heather's."

"Oh, I forgot you were going," Amy said from the kitchen as she put some bread in the toaster and then reached for a glass. Stepping to the doorway a minute later, she took a sip of her orange juice and asked, "What are you going to do at Heather's?"

"Probably work on cleaning out some boxes from her closets and doing some baking. There probably won't be much time to get outdoors there. What about you? Do you have plans for today?"

There was a pause as Amy brought her toast to the

table and reached for the butter. "Oh, I want to get outside and work in the garden. Adam said there was some weeding that could be done. And—" She laughed a little. "I think Sara would like a turn at the piano."

Mrs. Morgan joined in the laugh. "It sounds like a lovely day. You don't mind watching Danny and Jenny do you?"

Taking a drink before replying, Amy answered, "Of course not! Danny will probably dig for bugs and worms, and Jenny will want to pick every flower she sees. Oh, this is going to be a delightful day!"

Later that day, Amy came downstairs after settling her little charges in their beds for their afternoon naps. Sara sat at the piano. "You don't think my playing will bother them, do you?" she asked Amy anxiously.

Amy laughed and pushed back a stray piece of hair. "Piano music disturb them? After the last few days? No, I don't think so, unless you are going to play march music, then you might have Danny marching down the hall." She dropped down into a chair with a sigh. She'd spent all morning out in the garden and her back was tired. "What are you going to play?"

Sara was flipping through a stack of songbooks on the piano. "I don't know . . . Hmm, here's some old sheet music. Oh, I remember some of these songs."

"Play them."

"All right." The music was adjusted and Sara began. After playing it once through, she broke into song and sang the words as she played. It was a lovely tune and the words were quite sweet, but it was short. "This one is longer," Sara remarked, pulling another song before her.

Relaxing in her chair, Amy leaned back to listen. Sara had such a lovely voice. Suddenly her body tensed. That tune—what was it? Sometime, somewhere she knew she had heard that song. But where? When? Sara broke into song.

"I'll take you home again, Kathleen.
Across the ocean wild and wide,
To where your heart has ever been,
Since first you were my bonny bride."

Slowly Amy rose from her chair, her eyes fixed on the wall opposite and her hands clenching and unclenching at her side.

Sara was beginning the chorus.

"Oh! I will take you back, Kathleen,
To where your heart will feel no pain,
And when the fields are fresh and green . . ."

Breathing hard, Amy clasped her hands tightly together and pressed them to her lips. That song— What was it?

Sara continued singing, not noticing Amy's actions.

"I know you love me, Kathleen, dear,
Your heart was ever fond and true;
I always feel—"

An anguished cry from Amy broke the song off suddenly. "Matt! No! No! Oh, I remember! Matt!" she cried while tears coursed down her white face. "Kathleen, Matt! No, no!" Whirling blindly, Amy ran from the room, down the hall and out the front door.

Startled, Sara ran after her. "Amy!" she called. "Amy, come back!" Rounding the corner of the house, she stopped. Amy was running up the little path. Sara could still hear her cries. "But I can't leave the children!" she thought. Turning, she dashed back inside to the telephone. Quickly she dialed a number, watching out the window at Amy's form getting farther and farther away. "Oh, answer!" she pleaded silently.

"Hello?"

"Justin! Thank God you are there. You have to come home right away! She's remembered, and Mother's at town with Heather and Dad, and Adam's off— But the children are napping and I can't leave. She's going up the path! Oh, Justin, hurry!"

"Sara! What are you talking about? Calm down! Now, what happened?"

"I don't have time to tell you now. Just hurry! It's Amy! And the others are gone!"

"I'm on my way!"

As soon as Justin hung up, Sara replaced the receiver with a trembling hand. "Oh, Lord, please don't let Amy get hurt or lost! Bring Justin soon! Or Adam." Snatching up the phone again, Sara quickly dialed Heather's house. The story she told there was a little more coherent, and Heather said they would all start praying. "Should Mother come home?"

"I don't know. Justin's on his way here, but—oh, Heather, I don't want to be alone!"

"All right. Calm down, honey. We'll let Dad know and then head up, all right?"

Sara sniffed and nodded. Then, remembering that

Heather couldn't see her, added, "Yes."

When Justin, arriving before Sara thought was even possible, stepped from his truck, she raced to him. "She's gone up the path!"

Seldom had he seen his sister so upset, and Justin slipped an arm around her. "What happened?"

"I was playing and singing and suddenly she cried out for Matt and said, 'I remember!' and ran from the house."

"What song were you playing?"

"Umm, it was 'I'll take you back Kathleen', but Justin, hurry!"

Justin was torn. He knew he should go after Amy, but Sara was in such a state that he didn't want to leave her alone.

Sara's next words eased his fears for her.

"Heather said Mother was coming right home."

"All right." Justin gave his sister a quick hug. "Pray Sara and don't stop!"

Rapidly he started up the mountain slope, around the cabin and up the path. How far had Amy gone? What would she be like when he found her? These thoughts and many others raced through part of his mind while the other part was praying for help and wisdom.

There wasn't as much of a climb as he had feared. Upon reaching the bench which overlooked the valley, he found Amy crumpled up on the ground beside it sobbing bitterly. Dropping down beside her, he placed a gentle hand on her shoulder and whispered with compassion, "Oh, Amy!"

"He's gone!" was the heart-wrenching cry from the sobbing figure. "Matt!"

The wail was filled with an anguish Justin had never

seen before and it cut him to the heart. "Oh, Father, be with her," he whispered.

The light head raised and in tones of despair, her face ashen, Amy gasped, "Gone! They're all gone!"

"No, Amy! That's not true. Danny and Jenny are here, and Jesus Christ is with you. He won't leave you. He's here. I'm here."

Almost choking over a sob, Amy flung herself into Justin's arms and the tears flowed freely while he held her close. He couldn't say anything for a time, he was too much moved by her distress.

When at last the shuddering sobs, which had shaken the girl in his arms, had lessened, he began to quote comforting words. "I will never leave thee nor forsake thee. . . . When thou passest though the valley I will be with thee. . . . Yeah, though I walk through the valley of the shadow of death, I will fear no evil for Thou art with me. Thy rod and thy staff, they comfort me. . . . The Lord giveth and the Lord taketh away, blessed be the name of the Lord. . . . When my father and my mother forsake me, then the Lord will take me up. . . . Fear not for I am with thee. . . ."

At last Amy pulled away from the comforting arms and fumbled for her handkerchief. Before she found it, Justin had put his clean one in her hands. With her face hidden in its folds, she drew a long, tremulous breath and leaned against the seat of the bench.

"Come on," Justin said quietly, "sit on the bench. It will be easier."

Stiffly Amy rose and let him help her up. Once they were seated, Justin watching her with keen yet anxious eyes, Amy let her hands drop to her lap, revealing a face so changed that Justin reached for her pulse. He had no idea who "Matt" was and waited in silence for her to speak. "I remember everything now." Her voice was dull and almost lifeless. "I wish I had died in the crash."

~28~

"No, you don't, Amy," Justin countered firmly. "Think of Danny and Jenny. They would have died without you."

A flicker of something passed over her face and then was gone. Justin waited quietly for her to speak again. When she didn't, he asked softly, "Do you want to talk about it? It might help."

"Matt . . . was my brother. He was the best big brother anyone could ask for." She stared down into the valley. "Our parents died when I was small. I don't remember them much. Our uncle took us in and adopted us after a time."

Justin quickly realized why there had been a change of names, though he wondered if Jones was the real or adopted name.

"Matt fell in love with a really sweet girl and they got married. It was at a white church with a high steeple. The sky was blue and they rang the bell . . ." her voice died away into silence.

Watching her face, Justin saw the corners of her mouth turn up in a faint smile. He knew she was reliving the day. They were both so still that one sparrow, braver than the others, flew down almost to their feet and snatched a small bug. Then, tipping his head, he sang madly. Amy started and the sparrow darted away. The spell was broken and pain filled Amy's eyes once more.

"Only a few months after Matt and Kathleen were married, their house burned to the ground. But they were safe and found a new house in Santa Rosa. Danny was born there and then Uncle died. It was sudden and unexpected. Matt and Kathleen opened their home and took me in. There was no where else to go. Then Jenny was born. We were so happy together. Matt used to sing about the house. When he was in a playful mood, he'd sing, 'I'll take you back Kathleen' and she would laugh and tell him she wouldn't go back." Tears began to trickle down Amy's cheeks as she talked. "And then one day . . ." She bit her lip and her chin quivered. "One day . . . Oh! I can't bear it, I can't!"

Justin put his arm around her and she sobbed into his shirt front.

When she could finally speak again, she kept her face hidden. "There was an accident . . . A truck hit their car. . . . I was home with the little ones. . . . They were killed instantly." For several minutes she didn't speak as shudder after shudder ran through her frame. Justin felt them and his arm tightened about her shoulders.

"Then it was over. I kept the children. I was almost twenty. I just couldn't lose them too."

There were a dozen questions Justin wanted to ask when she stopped, but he couldn't. Not then. The poor girl had been through enough as it was. Perhaps later, after she had rested—

"But they claimed them. Said I couldn't keep them. I fought them off as long as I could."

Justin ventured one question. "Who?"

"Some relative of . . . Kathleen's. They live in Minnesota and had come for the . . . the funeral. Nothing was said then, but . . . I . . . I had to take them there or they would have come. They said they had . . . the right. We got on the plane, but we crashed." A violent fit of trembling swept over her at the remembrance.

Justin thought it was time to take up the story. "You all got out of the plane after the crash, but somehow you and the children became separated from the pilot and co-pilot. You wandered in the woods until the Lord led you to us."

"Yes." It was the faintest of whispers.

Justin didn't say anything. Right then he couldn't think of a single thing to tell the heartsick girl.

Amy straightened. A numbness had crept around her mind and, though her heart ached like never before, the numbness was easing it. Life would go on, it always did, even when she so desperately wished it wouldn't. Why was the sun shining? The whole world should be shrouded in gloom. Everyone who had ever been dear to her was gone, except Danny and Jenny, and they too would soon be gone. Now that everyone knew who they were, the relatives would come. "No!"

Her sudden, vehement exclamation startled Justin from his thoughts.

"They can't have them! If I'd never remembered, they would be safe. But I won't let them!" She began to shake, her hands clenched and her breath coming in short gasps. "They can't have them!"

"Amy, it is going to be all right." Justin realized she was in shock. He placed a hand over hers and said, "You are growing cold. Come on." He stood.

Looking up, Amy stared at him, her white face and her dark eyes filled with a haunting pain he would never forget. "Where?"

"I'm taking you home. The mountain air gets cool if you aren't doing anything."

But Amy shook her head listlessly; the momentary passion seemed but a brief spark. "I don't want to go back. What's the use? Almost everyone is gone and those left will soon be gone."

Standing directly in front of her, Justin said her name with such firmness that she looked up. "Christ is not gone. You are not alone. He will be with you now and forever. Can't you trust Him?" His voice had softened. "Can't you believe that He will work things out for good?"

"I want to, but, oh, it is so hard! I can't think anymore." Wearily she rubbed her hand over her eyes.

Justin pulled her to her feet. "Come on."

Too exhausted to argue or protest, too worn out to resist, Amy stumbled down the trail, her mind refusing to focus on anything. Had it not been for Justin's strong arm supporting her, she would have sunk down into the sweet, green grass, not caring if she ever got back up again or not.

It wasn't until Justin had seen Amy sleeping in her own bed and heard his mother whisper, "I'll stay with her, Son," that he slipped away and discovered the entire Morgan family gathered. Even Timothy and Heather were there. Sinking into a chair, he leaned his head on his hand and sighed. The clock struck four.

"What happened?"

Justin looked up. "Where are the children?" He didn't remember seeing any of them.

"Mrs. Douglas said she would watch ours and Dr. Douglas came up and took Danny and Jenny down to town," Heather answered. "We weren't sure what Amy would be . . . If she would . . ."

Justin nodded. He understood and was thankful there were no little ones around.

"Did she remember everything?" Sara's question was whispered and her face still showed signs of the strain her emotions had been in.

"Yes. I only have the bare facts, but it's enough to understand why her brain didn't want to remember." Slowly he told them what he had learned. By the time he was finished, Sara and Heather were both crying softly and even the men looked moved.

"That poor girl!" Heather sniffed.

"Oh, those relatives can't take Danny and Jenny from her!" Blinking back her tears, Sara sat up in her chair. "Dad, can't you do something?"

"I can talk to the police in Jackson," Adam said slowly, "but I don't know what that could do. But I don't want to see those two handed over to strangers."

Mr. Morgan frowned thoughtfully. "Is Amy twenty-one?"

Justin shrugged. "I don't know. She said something about being almost twenty at the funeral, but I have no idea when that was."

"Why didn't the relatives look for Amy and the children when they didn't arrive?" Heather demanded. "They must not want them very much. Who are the relatives anyway?"

"I don't know, but . . ." mused Justin in a voice that said he was deep in thought. The others waited patiently.

"I'll be back. I have a phone call to make." He stood, placed one hand on his pocket and then turned to his brother. "Adam, do you still have Rick McDonald's number?"

"It's in the office on Dad's desk."

"Thanks." Hurrying to the office, Justin soon found the number and dialed it. In a few minutes he was relating everything he knew to the F.B.I. agent who listened closely.

"Well, it's not much to go off of, but it will give us something to start on," Rick said. "You say she isn't well enough for more questions?"

"No, she's exhausted. When she is feeling better, I should be able to get more information to you, but I wanted to let you know what was going on."

The agent thanked him and said the information was helpful.

"I did have one other question, sir. Do you know if Amy will have to lose the children? It sounds like they are her only kin and she would be devastated over losing them."

The F.B.I. agent promised to look into the matter, and after a few more words, Justin replaced the phone and sat staring at the wall.

~29~

When Amy awoke, the room was dusky. She heard the soft murmur of voices coming from another room. Everything was quiet, peaceful, she felt safe. The thoughts from earlier came trooping in, the remembrance of the past that she had forgotten. The pain at the loss of her beloved brother was still there but it was duller, more subdued, not sharp and agonizing as it had been earlier. Turning her head, she saw Mrs. Morgan seated in a chair near her bed.

"Mother," she whispered.

Mrs. Morgan rose, and, stepping over, sat down on the edge of Amy's bed, her hand reaching up and smoothing back the light hair. "Yes, Dear, I'm right here."

"It hurts, here," and Amy pressed a hand over her heart.

Gently placing a hand on top of Amy's, Mrs. Morgan said, "I know it does, Child, but it does ease, the pain subsides and, though it may ache still, you can focus on the sweet memories."

Amy was still for several minutes. Her mind was tired. "Mother, I'm going to miss you and . . . and everyone."

"Miss us? Amy Child, what are you talking about?"

Amy's fingers began playing with the sheets, twisting them and bunching them. "I can't stay here now that I remember. I don't belong here. I'll have to find a job somewhere. I don't want to go back to Santa Rosa. And with the children gone—"

Mrs. Morgan wouldn't let her go on. Placing a hand over Amy's lips, she shook her head. "No, Amy, you are not going away. Not unless you really want to. This is your home, we are your family, and you belong right here. And I wouldn't think about losing Danny and Jenny yet. God placed you and them in our family, and we're not going to give any of you up without a struggle."

Tears filled Amy's eyes and overflowed onto the pillow. "I . . . I don't have to go away? You . . . you don't want me to leave? Oh, Mother!" She held out her arms and felt Mrs. Morgan gather her close. There, sheltered in the arms of the only mother she had ever really known, Amy wept. This time the tears were less bitter, and she felt comforted knowing that she was wanted and could call the Morgan cabin, *home.*

When the tears ceased to flow, Mrs. Morgan eased the girl back onto her pillow. Bending, she kissed her and whispered, "Even as a mother comforteth her children, even so will I comfort you, sayeth the Lord."

Amy could only smile faintly. That verse had been read only the other day at the table.

There was a step outside and the soft light from the hall spilled into the room as the door was quietly opened. Mrs. Morgan turned. "She's awake, Justin."

Stepping over to the bed, Justin looked down at the tearstained face, laid a finger on her pulse and then asked, "How are you feeling?"

Amy tried to smile. "It still hurts, but—" Tears spilled

from her eyes and she pressed her lips tightly together.

"Are you hungry?"

Glad she could answer without speaking, Amy shook her head.

"Would you like some tea?"

Another shake of the head.

Justin smiled. He knew Amy didn't care much for tea. "I'm going to bring you a glass of milk and I want you to promise me you will try to drink it."

Amy nodded. She was thirsty.

Someone must have been waiting in the hall with the milk, for Justin wasn't gone long enough. He seemed pleased when she eagerly drained the glass and then lay back with a sigh, her eyes closed. "Try to sleep again, Amy," Justin ordered softly before slipping away, leaving his mother beside the bed.

"Mother," whispered Amy, a few minutes later, opening her eyes. "Mother, have you sung the evening hymns?"

"No, Dear."

"Please, would you? I'll be all right alone a little while. Please. I want to hear them."

"Are you sure you'll be all right?" Mrs. Morgan hesitated about leaving her. But Amy was positive.

Moments later, as the strains of the first song drifted in on the still evening air, Amy relaxed.

"God, that madest earth and heaven,
Darkness and light;
Who the day for toil has given,
For rest the night."

Drawing a long sigh, Amy turned and nestled into the pillow. A verse she had read only that morning came back to her. "It is vain for you to eat the bread of sorrows, for so, He giveth his beloved sleep." Sleep. "I won't worry any more, Lord," she whispered. "I'll try not to even think." Then, exhausted, weary, and worn out, Amy's eyes closed and she slept.

It was nearly noon when Amy ventured into the living room the following day. Her face was still pale, but there was a peace in her eyes and a calmness in her manner that gave evidence of a Help not given by earthly wisdom. Justin and Sara looked up as she entered and Justin quickly rose.

"Come and sit down, Amy."

Amy gave a small smile. "You don't have to fuss over me now, Justin," she said. "I'll be all right. You were right. Jesus Christ has not left me." She sat down on the couch with Sara. Tears filled Amy's eyes, but she turned to her and whispered, "Thank you!"

"Fo . . . for what?" Sara stammered. "I brought you so much grief, I—"

"No, Sara," Amy countered, seizing her hands. "If you hadn't played that song, I wouldn't have remembered. But now . . . I know who I am and where I came from. Yes, the past hurts and it's hard to remember all those happy times, but I can heal now. Before, I wasn't . . . well, I didn't feel whole, but now I do. The part of me that was missing has been found. And I thank you."

Sara couldn't say anything, but there was no need. The two girls embraced each other, their tears mingling.

Justin appeared with Mrs. Morgan and a plate of toast. "I want you to eat something," he directed, setting a tray across Amy's lap. "You haven't had anything to eat since lunch time yesterday."

Amy made no objection. She didn't feel hungry, but she knew the others would worry over her if she didn't eat, and they had worried enough. When her simple meal was over, she looked around the room in a puzzled way. "Where are Danny and Jenny?"

Mrs. Morgan handed the empty tray to Sara and replied, "They are staying with Heather and Timothy for a time." She lowered her voice to a confidential tone. "Justin didn't want their noise to disturb you, and Danny was excited about staying with Lucas and Brandon."

"They wouldn't disturb me. They couldn't." She leaned back. "When are they coming home? I want to see as much of them as I can before they have to go—" She bit her lip and blinked rapidly, fighting the tears which again threatened to spill.

"Amy," Justin said firmly, "Danny and Jenny are staying with you."

"But—"

"Just listen a minute. We got a phone call only a few hours ago from an F.B.I. agent who has been trying to find out who you were and where you belonged. Yesterday, after your memory returned, I passed on the information to him and asked about the children. I'm not sure how he did it all, but he found the lawyer who handled all your brother and sister-in-law's affairs. It turns out that your brother made a will only a few days before he died. The children, and everything else, were left to you if anything happened to him and Kathleen. Kathleen's relatives have no claim on them."

"But—"

"The lawyer tried to tell you this," Justin went on, ignoring her interruption, "but you must have been in a state of shock still and didn't understand it. The relatives didn't look for you because they had heard about the will and knew that, even in court, you would probably win, so they gave up. You didn't tell them you were bringing the children, did you?"

Amy shook her head.

"That's why no one was looking for you after the crash."

"Then I don't have to lose them?"

Mrs. Morgan laid a hand on her arm, "No, Dear, you never have to worry about giving them up."

Amy drew a long breath and let it out slowly as though a heavy band which had been pressing her heart was suddenly released. "Thank you, Father," she whispered with a full heart.

That evening the Morgan family were gathered around the large living room in the Morgan cabin. Jenny was in Amy's arms and Danny was in Grandpa's lap. Timothy and Heather had just left and everyone was silent for a few minutes.

Looking over at Amy, Justin noticed a worried look begin to creep across her face. "What is it, Amy?" he asked.

"Do I have to go back to Santa Rosa and . . . and close the house and take care of things?" She glanced first at Justin and then around the room at the others, before coming back to Justin.

"Do you want to go?"

"No!" The answer was quick and decisive. "I don't think I could stand to go back. Not yet anyway. Perhaps some day I will want to, but not now."

Mr. Morgan spoke over Danny's brown head. "Would you like Adam and me to go and take care of things for you?"

"Oh, would you, Dad?" She turned to Adam questioningly after Mr. Morgan nodded.

"Sure, if you'll keep the garden weeded."

A relieved smile crossed Amy's face. She hugged Jenny closer and replied, "I would love to take care of the garden."

A yawn from Danny put a stop to the conversation and Justin rose to play the evening hymns while Sara remarked, "It's very nice to have you here, Amy, because now Justin comes up and plays the evening songs more often."

Amy smiled but made no reply. This was home. This was her family. The past was a memory, sweet and sad, but she couldn't live in the past. She was going to live in the here and now. All those storms had given her a gift she never dreamed of, family, love, and most of all, a new and better understanding of her Savior. With Christ beside her she could go on.

Epilogue

The mid-morning sun was warm that day in early summer. The chatter of young voices coming through the open windows of the house in town was proof that something unusual was happening. Carrying a watering can, a bright faced young woman stepped from the door and descended the porch steps. She hummed a tune as she watered the cheerful flowers blooming alongside the walk, pausing now and then to stoop and pull a stray weed.

"Amy!"

The woman turned and a bright smile crossed her face. "Good morning, Sara. Where is Alex? We're supposed to leave soon."

Sara tried to scowl but her merry face prevented more than a half frown. "He's still at the hospital. Wouldn't you know that on the day we have something planned, an accident happens and 'Dr. Wright must be called in to do surgery.' I knew I should never have married a doctor! Is Justin here?"

Amy laughed. "Not yet. Perhaps he was held up by the same accident."

Leaning against the white picket fence, Sara gave an exaggerated groan. "What made us fall in love with doctors, Amy? They're always late, and you can never be sure they'll show up for anything you plan!."

There was a twinkle in Amy's eyes as she replied, "You certainly had plenty of time to think of the consequences since it took you so long to agree to marry Alex. As for me, well—" Her smile broadened and her eyes fastened on the well known figure striding down the sidewalk.

Sara stepped aside as Justin came through the gate. "Do you know when Alex is coming?" she asked, after watching her brother kiss his wife.

Turning, Justin replied, "Yep, he said he'd be along in about ten minutes. Surgery didn't take as long as they thought it would." He wrapped his arms around Amy as he spoke.

"Sara was just complaining that we have busy husbands who are always late. I'm not sure she would know what to do if Alex were on time."

A general laugh sounded in the small front yard.

The screen door banged and a sweet voice called out, "Aunt Amy, where are Matt's shoes?"

"Did you ask Danny?" Justin called.

"Yes, well, I tried," Erin Louise answered, "but he's running around with Brandon and Lucas and isn't any help."

Tipping back her head, Amy looked up at her husband. "I'd better go and find them." Gently she pushed aside the arms about her and hurried up the steps. "Did you look on the bookshelf?" she asked as the screen door shut behind her with a soft thud.

Justin looked from the door to his sister. "Are you

waiting for Alex here?"

"That's the plan. Heather is already here, I see, and Timothy is meeting us later. I'm glad it's such a nice day; the children can be outside once we get to the cabin."

Justin laughed. "Yes, with Heather's five and our four, it makes things rather lively. But Mother and Dad won't mind."

Together, the brother and sister strolled up the walk to the porch where the sound of excited voices assaulted their ears.

"How Amy manages to make time to do any gardening with four youngsters is still a puzzlement to me," Sara paused to remark, eyeing the watering can resting on the table outside the front door.

"Don't forget Danny had just turned four when we were married and Jenny was close to two."

"And now Danny is almost eight," Sara said musingly. "It's hard to believe."

Justin didn't have time to reply, for at that moment an active young boy caught sight of him. With a shout of "Daddy!" he raced for the door, charged through it and flung himself into Justin's waiting arms.

"Are we going to Grandpa's now, Daddy, are we?"

With a laugh, Justin set the boy back on his feet and stepped inside. "As soon as everyone's ready we will. Why don't you run up and see if Mama has found Matt's shoes."

"I know where they are. I kicked 'em under my bed instead of putting them away yesterday," and with those candid parting words, Danny tore out of the room.

Justin shook his head while Sara laughed.

The noise level in the house only seemed to increase as Heather tried to collect all her children and Amy gathered what baby things she might need for a trip with little Kathleen. Justin tried to help, but the phone rang and he was stuck listening to a patient complain of an imaginary illness. Finally Sara took pity on everyone and, seizing Danny in one hand and Brandon in the other, marched them outside, calling, "We're starting up the mountain!"

In an instant, Erin Louise, toting her little sister on her hip, hurried out after them, followed by Jenny and Lucas, leaving Matt sitting on the floor wailing because his shoes weren't on.

Outside, Sara marched the children up the sidewalk and then back down, turning around once again only to meet Dr. Wright coming down the street. At sight of him, Sara forgot about the children and rushed to greet him.

Finally all the children were packed into the cars and the whole caravan was off up the mountain.

"You know, Justin," Amy said softly as she gazed at the lovely mountain slopes, "almost every time we come up here, I remember the first time you drove me up to the cabin. Do you remember? You had just released me from the hospital, and I was nervous."

Glancing over at her with a smile, Justin reached a hand out and placed it over Amy's. "I think of that time now and then too. But what I think of even more is when you said 'yes' to a certain question."

Amy blushed. "But that wasn't the first time we were up at the bench together."

"No," Justin agreed, turning into the driveway, "but it's my favorite time to remember."

Pulling up before the cabin, he saw his mother coming out on the porch and waving, and he knew his dad and Adam were around someplace.

As the cars stopped, doors were flung open and the children tumbled out shouting, "Happy birthday, Grandma!"

Mrs. Morgan, beaming with delight, opened her arms and embraced each of the noisy youngsters.

"Where's Grandpa?" Brandon demanded.

"And Uncle Adam?" added Danny.

"Where's the puppy?"

"Yes, Grandma, where's the puppy?" several echoed the question.

"Adam has the puppy out behind the house, I'm sure Grandpa—" Mrs. Morgan's sentence was left unfinished, for the grandchildren had all scampered away, Matt trotting after them on his sturdy little legs, always last but always trying to keep up.

"Happy birthday, Mother," Justin said, bending down to kiss her. "Hope you don't mind a lively bunch today. I think everyone is a little on the wild side."

"Speak for yourself, Just," Sara teased, giving her brother a friendly push so she could hug her mother. "You should have heard the commotion going on at his house before we came up here." Sara shook her head.

Mrs. Morgan laughed. "Did you add to the noise, Sara?"

Sara pretended to look astonished at the very idea and Amy came to her rescue.

"Actually she was a big help, Mother." She handed Baby Kathleen to Mrs. Morgan as she added, "She took them all outside—"

"Except for Matt," Heather broke in to say. "Poor little guy. He was left with no shoes on and was sure he would be left behind."

"He's always getting left behind," Alex grinned. "But just watch, one of these days he'll be in the lead. Happy birthday, Mother."

Mrs. Morgan smiled at the chuckle that went around, accepted the greeting of her newest son-in-law and then asked, "Are we going to go inside or stay out?"

"You all can do whatever you like, but Amy, Sara and I are going to go make lunch. If we don't, we will not be responsible for the tears." Heather opened the screen door and stepped in followed by Sara, while Amy paused long enough to kiss her baby daughter.

The afternoon was filled with laughter. The children played out on the sun-warmed mountain slope, Adam took Amy on an inspection of the garden, and Grandpa read stories in the shade of a tree to Matt, whose little legs had grown tired, and Anne, after Erin Louise was tired of toting her little sister around. Timothy appeared in the middle of the afternoon, and soon after, the ladies disappeared inside to prepare supper. Mrs. Morgan was not allowed to help, and the three girls enjoyed their time together in the kitchen.

Evening found the entire Morgan family gathered in the living room. The night ait was chilly and Adam had built a fire. It was cozy there and a quietness descended on the room. Mrs. Morgan had opened her gifts before supper and now everyone was relaxing silently. Even the younger children, worn out from their various activities outdoors, seemed content to nestle in someone's lap or lean a tired head against a knee or shoulder. Amy, from her sheltered place in the circle of Justin's arm, with her youngest child sleeping peacefully in her lap, looked about the room. It had taken Dr. Wright quite some time to persuade Sara to marry him, but at last she had given in and they had been married early that spring. They looked so happy together and it was pleasant to have Sara living in town.

Over on the other couch, Heather sat with her Timothy on one side and Erin Louise on the other. As usual, Erin Louise held Anne in her lap. As the only daughter, she had been delighted with the arrival of a little sister and included Anne in as many things as she could. Heather and Timothy's other children, Brandon, Lucas and Silas, along with Danny, were scattered about the room, lying on the rug or lounging in chairs, while Jenny claimed the seat of honor on Grandma's lap.

Giving an involuntary sigh of contentment, Amy tilted her head and smiled up into her husband's eyes. There was no thought of that night more than four years ago when she had first arrived, sick, injured and in desperate need of a family.

"Since everyone is here," Mrs. Morgan spoke, glancing around at her children and grandchildren, "would someone please play the evening songs? Justin? Sara? Amy?"

"You play, Just," Sara said. "I can't play one handed." She held up her right hand clasped in her husband's.

"Amy?" Justin looked down at his wife. But she shook her head. Standing up, Justin crossed to the piano and sat down. After running his fingers over the keys and trying out a chord here and there while the family gathered about, he began the first hymn. No one needed the words to the songs, they were as familiar to each one as their own name.

The room grew dim and the glowing pink clouds seen out the large window faded as the sun went down. The final lines of the last hymn died away on the still evening breeze which moved the curtains softly.

"Abide with me till in Thy love
I lose myself in hean'n above."

"Dad," Justin said quietly without stirring from the piano bench. "Will you pray before we head back home?"

39872915R00150

Made in the USA
Middletown, DE
27 January 2017